Butcher

The *Devil Souls* Motorcycle Club

LeAnn Ashers

dedication

This is for everyone who is waiting for their own unusual, unpredictable, and crazy kind of love. May you find your own Butcher. <3

Who says love must be sane?

Butcher

one

Shaylin

I'm having dinner at Blue's Steak House in Raleigh, Texas. I moved here three years ago to open a bakery. My hometown is small, but it already had a thriving bakery, so here I am—and my establishment is getting more business every year.

My brother, Lane, is the president of the Grim Sinners. My father started the club, and it has thrived. I grew up around these gruff, protective men. They may be rough, but they have a soft spot for those they care about.

I am the princess of the club because, for some crazy, unknown reason, I am the only girl. None of the other members has a daughter, only sons. The only reason my dad allowed me to move to this town is because the Devil Souls MC is here. They are close friends with my dad's club. Like the Grim Sinners, the Devil Souls has me under their protection.

I know something is going down with the clubs right now, and I have to be careful. I am not allowed to know the details— that is a huge part of me staying safe. The clubs are legit, so if something is going down, something bad must have happened.

Something went down a couple of months ago that rocked our family. My brother has a daughter, Tiffany. We knew nothing of this and he didn't either. When the Devil Souls was taking down a trafficking ring, they found his daughter there.

They called my brother and the rest was history. The mother was going to use her for ransom, and then she dropped off the face of the earth.

Well, almost.

Grinning to myself, I look around the room thinking back to when I last saw Tiffany's mother. I was driving down the road, and I saw her walking along the sidewalk. What did I do? I followed her to her apartment. I watched her walk inside, and I followed her.

I burst through the door and spotted a plate sitting on a table beside the broken-down couch. I picked it up and slammed it over her head, and she slumped onto the floor, unconscious. I walked back down the stairs, got into my car, and went to work.

I am not someone who fights people, but that woman deserved it. In fact, she deserved worse. She treated my niece horribly—that little girl went through hell because of her.

The room falls silent, and I turn around to see what's going on. The Devil Souls MC and my brother's club, the Grim Sinners, file into the room and gather around a long table.

That's when I see him.

He is tall, probably around six five, tattooed to the walls. His arms, neck, and back are covered in tattoos. His hair is cut short on the sides and long on the top. He has stubble all along his jaw bone. He is intimidating. I like that, and just from the side view I am attracted to him.

I don't take my eyes off him as he walks around the table so his back is facing the wall. He scoots in and my heart starts pounding, waiting for him to look at me.

His head turns and his eyes connect with mine.

His eyes darken and his nose flares.

Oh shit.

He is handsome in a very rough and rugged way. This man is dangerous—he gives off this raw power, and his eyes are dark and seem to look into my soul.

A few minutes later, the waitress hands my menu back to me. A piece of paper is taped to the back, and a phone number is scribbled on it. I look up and see him smirking at me.

The guy growls more loudly and scoots his chair out. I know alpha males, and this man is the ultimate one.

Handing back the piece of paper with the number, I shake my head and the waitress walks away. The guy looks seriously pissed off. Winking at him, I stand up and grab my purse off the back of my chair. I smile at him and then at my brother, who is staring at both of us. I smirk at Butcher and walk out of the room. As I'm heading out the door, I hear a chair hitting the floor. Grinning, I get in my car. My phone dings and I see a text from Lane.

Lane: Behind you.

Butcher walks out the front door of the restaurant, his eyes on me. I start the car and back out, before pulling out onto the highway. I hear a motorcycle start up, and I look out my window. The guy is following close behind. Laughing, I turn on the radio and ignore him.

I probably shouldn't ignore this man, because following someone isn't normal, but nothing in the MC world is normal.

I am on break and I need to go back to my bakery, which is right down the road from Blue's. Shaylin's Sweets. How original, right?

ME: What's his name?

Lane: Butcher

Well, that's a different name for sure. Looking at my rearview mirror, I notice that he is so close to the back of my car that if I hit my brakes he would slam into me.

It seriously makes me wonder what this man wants. MC men are totally different from your everyday man. These men are a different breed altogether, and I feel like this Butcher is on a whole different level from them.

When I step out of my car in front of the bakery, I see Butcher pulling in. I stand still and watch as he pulls in right beside where I am standing. Butcher turns the bike off and stares at me intensely. He doesn't say a word, but we begin a staring match. I gulp and open my mouth to say something but close it instantly. *What do I say to this? What do I do? Do I tell him to leave?* But I feel like that won't work. I've got to admit that I find him extremely attractive. I have a thing for bad boys, and this man isn't a boy but something else entirely—which makes it so much better.

So I don't say anything. I turn around and walk straight through the front door of my bakery. Mary, one of my workers, pops out from the back, takes off her apron, and hangs it on the hook. "I am going to lunch now," she says without looking at me. Mary is my best friend. We have been friends since I was a baby. Her mom used to watch me when my dad was busy. Usually I was taken to the club with him, and one of the other MC men, who I call my uncles, would watch me.

Mary finally looks up at me and smiles, then her eyes pop open and she drops her purse. I crane my neck around to see what's the matter.

Butcher.

He is standing behind me, and I can see why she would have a reaction like that. He doesn't look like a cuddly teddy bear. This man looks like he could kill you with his pinky—hell, if his permanent glare didn't kill you first.

"You will be okay?" She lowers her voice almost to a whisper. Her eyes go from me to Butcher, who hasn't moved.

I smile and nod. "Yes, I will be fine. Go on."

She nods and walks past us, her head down as she passes him. Mary may be my best friend, but she hasn't been around the MC life like I have. She saw them in passing, but that was really it. She was never someone who wanted to be a part of that life.

I watch as she hurries to her car, and I laugh under my breath. Butcher still hasn't taken his eyes off me. I don't even think he blinks. I walk into the kitchen to start a birthday cake. I gather the ingredients and measure everything out before setting it down on the counter. I place all the wet ingredients in the mixer before adding all of the dry.

I feel like I am being watched. I peer over my shoulder, and I jump at the sight of Butcher sitting in a chair next to the entrance to the kitchen. His eyes are still on me and he doesn't move.

I go back to working on my cake. This man is intense. Very intense. He doesn't say anything—the only thing he does is stare and stare. I want to say so much and, most of all, I want to ask what the eff he is doing.

I pour the batter into the floured cake pans and slip them into one of my many ovens. I stand back and clap my hands together to rid them of extra flour before heading to the sink to wash up.

I love this place. It's everything I dreamed of—and I got it. I went to school for years, perfecting my craft. I have been baking and cooking since I was a small kid, I used to stand in a chair so I could reach the counter. I know my concoctions were far from edible back then, but my father and brother never complained. I even took my baked goods to the clubhouse, and all my "uncles" claimed they were the best thing they'd ever tasted. Big softies, every single one of them.

Butcher still hasn't moved. The bell above the door dings as someone walks inside. I untie the string behind my back and slip my apron over my head before hanging it on the hook on the wall beside the door.

I walk out of the kitchen to the front of the bakery. Henry is standing in front of the counter. Henry is someone I can't describe. I get major creepy vibes, because he is like a dog panting over me. I feel like he is harmless, but he is annoying nonetheless.

"How can I help you today, Henry?" I ask him and he gets this excited look on his face. I would find it kind of endearing if he weren't covered in a year's worth of grime with some suspicious brown stains on his hands and other parts of his body. I don't want to think of that right now. I have a really weak stomach, and I can't stand any kind of bodily fluids.

Butcher is standing at the entrance to the kitchen. His eyes aren't on me, for once, but on Henry.

"I want a red velvet cupcake."

I open the glass and pull out his cupcake. I put it neatly inside a box and set it on the counter. As Henry reaches into his pocket for money, I am cringing inside. The crotch of his pants is wet. *Please let that be water.*

As I reach forward to take the money from him, he grins. I shudder at the sight of his tooth. Yes, tooth—because most of his are missing. He grabs my hand in a tight grip. I want to vomit as I take in his fingernails. *Don't puke, Shay,* I tell myself.

"Let me go," I tell him sternly. I spot Butcher, out of the corner of my eye, thundering up to the counter. I attempt to pull my hand free. "Let. Me. Go."

"No."

1, 2, 3…

Fuck it. I grab the tip jar off the counter and smash it on Henry's head. His eyes roll into the back of his head, and he hits the ground with a thump.

Butcher stares down at Henry, and my eyes widen as I see the grin on his face.

I smile back sweetly. "He should have let me go."

Butcher's grin widens and my stomach flips.

"Now what do I do with him?" I take out my phone to call Lane.

A hand closes over my cell phone. "I'll handle this," Butcher says in his gruff voice. I stare into his intense eyes. He lets go, and he grabs Henry's leg and proceeds to drag him through the kitchen.

I blink a few times and rush after him to see what he is going to do. Light shoots into the room as he opens the back door. I wince as he drags Henry across the concrete. Talk about road burn. Well, I did break a jar over his head—why am I worrying about that now?

Butcher continues dragging Henry without a care in the world, like he just taking an everyday stroll through the park. He drags him behind a building and moves plastic bags, along with debris, around him so he can't be seen.

Butcher turns around and stalks back to me. Every single step is filled with intent. His eyes never leave mine as he gets closer and closer.

I duck inside the building and go back to the front of the bakery, where a few more customers are drifting in. I take care of them and Mary walks in. The door shuts behind her, and she looks around like she is looking for someone.

I feel Butcher move close to me, and her eyes widen. She ducks her head and all but runs into the kitchen to be as far away from us as possible. Looking out of the corner of my eye, I see Butcher staring at the kitchen door.

I take that moment to look at him. He is all dark features and he is just *big*. He is buff and has this rough and tough exterior, but I know there is more to this man than what meets the eye.

When Butcher looks back in my direction, I quickly look away and go back to work, rearranging the showcase counter to make sure everything looks nice and orderly.

For the next couple of hours, people come and go, getting their desserts while booking cakes and cupcakes for weddings, birthday parties, and other celebrations. Butcher is now sitting in a chair just to the right of me. He intimidates everyone who walks into the room.

Mary hasn't come out of the back since she got back to work. It's close to closing time, and I'm starting to get hungry. I open the glass showcase, grab the rest of the vanilla cupcakes, and place them in a box. I grab the box and sit down in the chair next to Butcher, who is still staring at me. I hold a cupcake toward him. "Want one?" I blush. His lips turn up at the corners just slightly.

He takes the cupcake from me, his fingers brushing mine. I blush harder and look down. Licking my lips, I grab my own cupcake. I peel back the paper and take a bite.

Butcher peels back the wrapper of his cupcake and stuffs the whole thing in his mouth. Laughter bubbles up as I watch this man stuff his face with cupcakes—why is it so funny to see such a rough man eating a cupcake?

I take another out of the box and hand it to him. He winks and I jerk in shock. My mouth pops open a bit. *Did he just wink at me?* I smile at him, teeth and all. I probably look like a loon.

"Shaylin, I am going to start cleaning up!" Mary calls from the kitchen.

"Okay! I will be there in a second." I hand the rest of the cupcakes to Butcher, who immediately grabs another. I smile. I love seeing someone savor my cupcakes or anything else I make.

For the next hour, Mary and I clean everything up, along with preparing for tomorrow. Tomorrow is my day off, so I want to make sure everything is perfect for her and the other worker who will be here.

"Bye, Mary!" I walk Mary to the door and watch as she gets inside her car safely and drives away. I turn around and run face first into something hard. I back up—I ran into Butcher. His hand is on my forearm, steadying me.

"I've just got to lock up and make sure everything is off." I spin on my heel and go into the kitchen. I do a walk through to make sure all the refrigerators are closed and everything is turned off.

I turn off the light and walk back into the main room, and I see Butcher is already outside the door staring inside. By the time I've finished turning off the lights and locking up, Butcher is on his bike. *Okay then.* As I'm getting in my car, he is still staring at me. There is so much I want to say.

Swallowing, I sit in the driver's seat and put the key in the ignition. I feel my mind going in a million different directions. I pull out of the parking lot, and my eyes flick to the rearview window. I stop at the stoplight, and my eyes follow Butcher as he comes up on the right. The light turns green, and I turn left toward my house. Butcher turns in the other direction.

Well, I guess that is that. What did I expect? I honestly didn't know what to expect with him. One part of me had anticipated that he would follow me home, and the other side had thought he would part ways with me once I got off work.

Today has just been a weird day in general. I broke my tip jar over a man's head, even though he asked for it. Then Butcher dropped him behind a dumpster.

We aren't normal, but isn't normal overrated?

two

The Next Day

Beep! Beep! Beep! I groan and roll over in bed to turn off the alarm. Once it's turned off, I roll onto my back and yawn, my eyes watering. Then I reach onto the nightstand and grab my phone. I see a text

Lane: Your niece wants to have a girl's day.

I grin at the prospect of spending the day with my niece. I love that little girl more than anything. She had a rough go of it before Lane got her. I want to kill her mother, and I would have if I thought I could get away with it. What kind of mother tries to put her kid up for ransom?

Me: Be there in an hour.

Lane: Perfect.

Thirty minutes later, I am ready. I will get breakfast with my niece. I grab my purse off the back of the chair and my keys off the table. I push my hair out of my face and behind my ear as I put on my shoes. All of my shoes are flats because I can barely walk on solid ground. I am clumsy. That was a huge thing for me while growing up. I have broken way too many bones because of it. I step onto the porch and lock the door behind me, slinging my purse higher up on my shoulder. That's when I see something lying on my lawn chair.

What the actual fuck is going on? Is some crazed man or woman sleeping in my yard? I look around to see what I can knock some heads with, and all I see is a rock. Shrugging, I bend down and grab the rock. I raise my hand and chuck it at the person lying on the lawn chair.

It hits them in what looks like the chest area. This person stands up, knocking the chair over, with a gun pointed directly at me. My eyes take in this person and I sigh loudly.

It is Butcher. It's official. This man is stalking me. I can't believe he actually slept in a chair in my yard. Who does this?

"What are you doing, Butcher?" I ask him and take a couple of steps closer. He doesn't say a word, but he does stare at me. "Butcher?" This time he looks me up and down before giving me that smile.

Okay then!

"I got to go…"

He nods and turns his back to me. He walks over to his bike and, for a few seconds, I blink in slight disbelief at what is happening. Okay. I am so confused. If this man wants to date me or something, he has it way backwards. But I must also admit he is totally different from every other man out there.

First of all he is scary to look at, but I find that attractive.

I back up a few steps, without taking my eyes off him, before walking through my yard to my car. I live in the suburbs. My father wanted me out in the country, but I didn't want to drive forty-five minutes to work every day.

As I put the key in the ignition, I see Butcher is still sitting there. I guess he is waiting on me. I pull away from the curb, make a U turn, and drive away.

My brother lives almost thirty minutes away from me, in a housing development near town. All the houses in the development belong to the MC. It's fenced and heavily guarded.

My brother had these houses built once he became president. What can offer more protection than having all your brothers together in one area? My father made the club thrive and do very well. My brother is what made it prosper. He used that business degree he got after he came home from his deployments from the military. Now they own close to fifty businesses throughout Texas and other states.

I hear a motorcycle speeding up behind me, and I look out my side window. Much to my surprise, it's Butcher. He is close to the back of my car. I guess he is coming along for the ride.

I pull up outside my brother's driveway and put in the code. The gate opens and I drive down the long driveway. I hear the bike turn off. I look out the rear window and see Butcher has parked outside the gate.

I pull up near the front porch, and Lane comes outside with my niece, Tiffany, on his back. He is babying her and she eats that up. Not that I blame her. Lane is an amazing father and, from the moment that little girl came into his life, everything changed for him. She changed all of our lives.

I climb out of my car and smile at Lane and my niece. My brother smiles back, and his head snaps up to look at his gate. I guess he sees Butcher. Lane's eyebrows shoot up and I shrug. I don't have an answer for him.

Tiffany tells Lane she wants down, and he sets her on the ground. "Bye, Daddy!" She hugs his hip because that's within her reach. A blinding smile comes over his face, and he presses his palm to the back of her head. "Love you, baby girl." She lets go of him and runs down the steps and straight into my car. I guess she is ready to go.

"Why is Butcher outside of my gate?" Lane asks as soon as Tiffany shuts the door.

I let out a loud breath and look at Butcher before answering. "Since yesterday, he hasn't left. He sat and watched me work all day yesterday then slept outside of my house."

Lane's eyes widen and he bursts out laughing. The smile drops from my face. *What is he laughing at?* I narrow my eyes at him. I don't like to be at the butt end of jokes.

Lane takes in my expression and immediately shuts up. "This man is fucking crazy and looks like he is stalking you. If I didn't know Butcher, I would put a bullet in his head for stalking you." He starts laughing again.

He is pissing me off. Butcher isn't crazy—he is just different. I take a step closer, ready to throttle him. Lane backs up. "You're crazy too, Shay. You blind people with all of that sweet shit and, bam, the crazy comes out."

I grin because I've got to admit it's true and he knows all about it. "That's right. I am going to go! I will see you later."

I climb in the car and roll down the windows. This is my and Tiffany's thing. We blast the radio and have all of the windows down. "Bye, Daddy!" Tiffany yells out the window, and she blows him a kiss. His face softens and he waves bye.

"Let's hit it Shay Shay!" She claps her hands, a huge smile on her face with those huge dimples on either cheek. I love that little girl!

I turn in the yard and blast the radio. She sings along with every word, and this little girl can't sing at all, but that doesn't stop us.

I wish my mom were around. She died from cancer when I was little, and I don't have any memories of her. I wish I had moments with her to remember. Lane remembers her some but not a lot. It saddens me that Tiffany had a mother who is a waste of fucking air.

The gate opens automatically and I drive out. I pull straight onto the highway and Butcher pulls out behind us. "Who is that?" Tiffany asks and I look through the rear window. "A friend."

"Oh cool!" she says simply and doesn't ask any more questions. The bike revs up, and Butcher drives up beside Tiffany. She laughs and reaches her hand out. Butcher grins at her and touches her hand. She laughs even harder.

I grin at their antics.

We arrive at the mall. "Wait on me to come get you, angel," I tell Tiffany because she likes to do things herself. My door opens and I jump in shock. Butcher is standing there holding my door open. *Okay.*

I grab my purse off the passenger seat and walk around the car to let Tiffany out. She already has herself unbuckled. She steps out and latches onto my hand. Together we walk hand in hand into the mall, and Butcher walks about ten feet behind us.

Tiffany spots the nail place first thing and drags me there first. She leads me right up to the counter. "I need to get my toenails painted. Dad tried last night and it didn't end well," she explains and at that I look down at her toes. It takes everything in me not to start laughing. Her whole toe is almost blue.

"How can I help you guys today?" the lady at the counter asks.

"We want two pedicures," I tell her and she points to the seats. Tiffany lets go of my hand and runs over to the one that is made for princesses, which is pink and gold with a crown resting at the top. She climbs in the seat and I sit down beside her.

Everyone stops talking, and I look to see what is going on. Butcher walks past me to the seat directly beside me. I lick my lips and stare at him. The lady who seated us is looking at us nervously as she wipes her hands up and down her clothes. She strides over to him. "Do you want a pedicure also?" Butcher glares at her like he can't even believe she asked that. She steps away and stumbles, hitting another man who works there. He catches himself and her. She apologizes and runs back the counter.

"Tiffany, go pick out a color for me and yourself—okay, sweetheart?"

She runs to the wall that is just nail polish. I sink back in my seat and grab the remote to turn on my back massager, keeping a close eye on Tiffany.

"So, do you want your toes done?" I ask Butcher, not knowing what else to say to him.

Butcher rolls his head around and stares at me. I guess that's the answer.

"I got you a red one!" Tiffany interrupts and hands me a bottle of red polish. She has a pink one for herself and one more: clear coat.

No, she isn't?

"I got a clear polish for him! Daddy lets me paint his all the time in this color." Lane is totally busted! Tiffany walks over to Butcher and sets the polish down in his lap. She smiles at him and goes back to her seat.

I grin and look over at Butcher. He is staring at the polish like it's going to come alive and attack him. I bite my lip to stop the laughter that is bubbling up. This is all too comical. "I am allergic," he blurts out.

I laugh loudly. That was epic. Tiffany leans forward and looks at him. "If you say so, Mr. Butcher!" she says in a sing-song voice.

His fingers wrap around the top of the polish, and he sets it down by his chair. Two ladies walk up to me and Tiffany, dragging two small chairs over. I sink into my chair.

"Shay, can we get some makeup today?"

I look over at Tiffany, and she looks at me with those huge eyes. "Of course!"

She grins at me and sits back in her chair. This little girl has everyone wrapped around her little finger. Who cares if Lane will probably kill me? It's just play makeup.

For the next thirty minutes, we are pampered. Once our toenails are dry, we step back into our sandals, and I walk over to pay for our stuff. The lady who freaked out earlier at the sight of Butcher shakes her head. "The scary man already paid."

Butcher is standing outside the nail place waiting on us. I take Tiffany's hand and walk straight to him. "Thank you! You didn't have to do that." He winks at me and my stomach flips.

Tiffany takes my cue. "Thank you, Mr. Butcher!"

She is too stinking cute!

Tiffany and I walk farther into the mall, and I see a clothing store that I absolutely love. I lead Tiffany inside and look for the little black dresses that I saw through the door. I grab a black one and the maroon one next to it. A woman can't have enough dresses. Tiffany has already spotted the little kids' section and is eagerly pulling me in that direction.

If the dresses don't fit, I will just bring them back. I let go of her hand and let her freely look. I may be a bit protective of her, but the thought of something happening to her has me very paranoid. Hell, it has every one of us paranoid. Tiffany is our world.

Tiffany picks out some dresses and shorts.

"Let's go try these on."

She nods and walks in front of me to the dressing room. I find one that is vacant and open the door for her. She steps inside, and I set my two dresses on a hook outside the door. The door slams shut.

"Which one do you want to try on next?"

She grabs a dress on top of the pile.

For the next ten minutes, we try on everything we selected, and we end up with two dresses and a pair of shorts. The girl loves her clothes. I open the door and, as we step out, I look at the hook where I had my clothes hanging.

These aren't my clothes—I can tell that at first glance. I take what is up there and unfold it. It looks like a dress an Amish woman would wear. What the heck? "Come on, Tiffany. Let's go grab my dresses. The saleslady must have put them back."

We walk over to where the rack of clothes was, and I see the whole rack is gone. *What the heck?* "I guess they are sold out?" I tell Tiffany. She smiles at something behind me, and I turn around to see what she is looking at—but there isn't anything there.

I arrive home around eight o'clock. Tiffany and I spend the day together. Butcher didn't get close to us, like he did at the nail salon, again. He was there, but he stayed out of the way. He just watched me.

I look behind me as I pull into my driveway, and I notice that Butcher isn't around. I guess he went home tonight. I yawn and step out of my car. I grab my bags and shuffle into the house. My feet are hurting something fierce. I can be on my feet all day at work and not hurt, but the moment I go to the mall, my feet kill me.

Once inside, I reset my alarm and lock the door. I go to my bedroom first and set the bags on the floor. I walk to my closet and grab a pair of shorts and a baggy T-shirt, and I take a hair tie off my wrist.

I walk into the kitchen and grab a bag of chips and water. I am so ready to veg out on the couch for the rest of the night while watching *Buffy the Vampire Slayer*. I grab a blanket off the back of the couch and tuck myself in.

I startle awake and look at the clock on the wall. Midnight. I fell asleep on the couch. I fold the bag of chips and set it on the coffee table. I walk to my front door to double check the locks before I settle in for the night.

I look out the window, and I see the same lawn chair that was in the yard earlier on the porch with Butcher lying on it. I go back to the living room and grab the blanket that I just used.

I open the front door slowly so I don't wake him up, and I walk over to him. His eyes are closed and, for the first time since I met him, he looks like he is at peace. I shake out the blanket and cover him with it.

I turn around and walk back into the house, and I lock the door behind me.

Butcher

She doesn't know I am awake as she covers me with a blanket. I can't leave her. The moment she is out of my sight, my body screams that it will be the last time I ever see her. I lost my family in a car accident, and since then I've kept everyone at arm's length besides my brothers.

My brothers became my family, and the military made me who I am. Shaylin surprised the fuck out of me. Her innocence, her sweet look, and the way the light radiates off her.

Sitting up on the lawn chair, I grab the blanket that has fallen halfway to the floor. I lift the blanket to my face and sniff, my eyes closing. It smells like her. I want her. I want her so fucking bad. I want to take her and hide her away so nothing can fucking hurt her.

At the bakery, when the guy touched her hand, I saw red. I wanted to tear him to fucking pieces just for touching her. I want to fucking kill anyone who even looks in her direction. When she was walking at the mall, men would stare at her, and I wanted to gouge their eyes out.

She is mine. She was mine the moment I laid eyes on her.

three

"Is he still following you?" Mary asks when she arrives at work. She must have seen Butcher sitting outside the bakery, staring inside. Today he seems much more intense.

"Yep." I set out the cupcakes in the glass showcase. Mary is staring at me like I am pure crazy.

"That doesn't freak you out?" She says slowly like I am illiterate.

I stand up and cross my arms across my chest. "Well, I guess it should, but it doesn't." I don't know what else to say to her because I sure as heck don't know what is going on.

"I say we have a girls' night tonight, and let's try to leave him behind?" Mary taps her hand on the counter, and I can tell she is nervous. I sigh and lean my hip against the counter. I guess a girls' night sounds like fun.

"Sure. What do you want to do?" I ask her as I turn back around to finish lining up the fresh cupcakes.

"The club?"

"Okay. Want me to pick you up tonight?".

"Yeah, as you're the D.D. I am in major need to let loose." I hear sadness etched into her voice, and that causes me to look at her with concern. I see bags under her eyes—she looks exhausted.

"What's wrong, Mary?" I touch her forearms. She hangs her head and lets out a deep breath that sounds like a sob.

"Mary?"

She looks up at me. "It's my stinking cousin again. I get calls almost every single night needing me to bail her out of parties that are getting too rough for her. She is getting into deep shit, and I don't want to deal with that." She stops and softens her voice, her eyes filled with tears. "She is family no matter what. I still remember her being my best friend while growing up."

I pull her into me, giving her a tight hug, taking some of the burden away. Her cousin got her into some deep shit a couple of years ago, and Mary was lucky to get out of it. Her cousin placed all the blame on her and said Mary would give the dealer the money.

"Call me next time and I will go with you," I say and she nods. I know Mary is scared because the dealer roughed her up and my dad got pissed. You can imagine what happened. Mary is my best friend and has been since I was a little girl. She is close to my dad and brother, but not the rest of the club. She just hasn't ever taken an interest in it.

"Thanks, Shay. I love you, it's just the stress is getting to me." She straightens up and smiles at me, tears streaming down her face.

"Welcome, doll." I smile saucily at her. "So, you ready to go out tonight? We got to find you a man!"

She throws her head back, laughing, before pointing a finger at herself. "Me? Look at you! You're still a v—"

I put my hand over her mouth before she says those words. "I think I got all the man I can handle." I look out the window at Butcher.

"Good point! I am going to work on the cake order for the birthday party later tonight."

"Thank you!" I call to her as she walks into the kitchen.

I think back to how Butcher loved my cupcakes, and I grab a to-go box. I fill it up and grab a bottle of water. "Mary, I am stepping out for a second," I yell as I reach the door. I step out and look at Butcher, who is focusing on me.

The Texas heat is blaring down on me when I step outside. So I know Butcher has to be frying in all of that black leather. He is sitting on his bike, though, like he is completely unfazed.

He is looking majorly badass today with those black eyes and dark hair. His eyes are so intense it's like he is staring deep into my soul, and they are scary as hell. His nose looks like it's been broken because it's slightly crooked. I can see, through his shirt, that tattoos cover his chest all the way up to his neck and his arms are both complete sleeves.

Once I am about a foot or so away from him, I stop. "I brought you some cupcakes." I smile at him widely. The expression in his eyes softens. I hand him the box and then the water. I lick my lips and get a good look at his face.

"Thank you."

A shiver runs up my back and leaves goose bumps across my arms. I am attracted to this man. I am attracted to bad boys. The more bad the better, and Butcher is as badass as it gets.

I smile at him again. "You're welcome."

I turn around and walk back toward the bakery. I may or may not have added extra pep to my step.

I walk inside Mary's house, which is just two blocks from where I live. It's eight o'clock and it's time to hit the club. I have to get back sort of early tonight because I have to work tomorrow. I've just got to open the store, and then I am coming back home to relax.

"Mary, are you ready?" I yell as I walk through her kitchen.

"Yeah!"

I walk into her living room, and I stop dead in my tracks at the sight of her cousin sitting on the couch dressed to the nines—in my dress! I let Mary borrow that, and I sure as hell don't want this girl in it!

"Hi, Shay. It's nice to see you!" Her cousin, whose name is Lexi, rises from the couch and walks over to me, and I notice immediately that she is way too thin. She has been on drugs for a while, and no amount of makeup can cover that. Drugs don't make someone a bad person, but the way some people act because of drug abuse creates trouble. This girl blinds people with that fragile look, and then she does shit.

So I cut right to the chase. "Why are you here, Lexi?"

Her eyes narrow, and then that smirk comes over her face. She knows I am not going to fall for her shit like her cousin does. Mary is too kindhearted and thinks the best of everyone, when she knows better.

"Whatever do you mean?" She mocks and flips her hair over her shoulder. It's like trying to flip tree trunks because it's that stiff.

I narrow my eyes on her. Is she joking? "Don't play me as a fool. I am not someone you want to mess with, Lexi. Don't screw over Mary. She is too good to you."

Lexi rolls her eyes and smacks her lips as she chews her gum. I cringe at the sound. "I can do whatever I want to do…" She smiles.

1, 2, 3, 4… I count to myself with my eyes closed so I don't pummel the bitch.

She finishes her sentence. "Bitch"

She went there.

My right fist shoots out, nailing her right on the mouth. One, I want her to shut the eff up, and two, I can't stand that gum chewing. Lexi grabs her nose.

"I told you not to mess with me, Lexi!" I have a temper—have I mentioned that already? Plus she was asking for it. I take a step closer to Lexi. "Now, are you going to be a good girl and not screw with Mary?" I say sweetly.

"Fuck that."

The smile falls from my face, and I grab a handful of hair with my right hand while my left clamps around her mouth so she doesn't make a sound. Even though Mary is tired of her cousin, I don't think she wants to see me manhandling her.

I drag her to the door and, much to my surprise, it opens. Butcher is standing there with a shit-eating grin on his face. I pull Lexi's hair and push her out of the house. She stumbles but stays on her feet. I step onto the porch, shutting the door silently. "Remember what I said!" I smile at her widely.

She gives me an evil look, and I just wave at her. Butcher is standing behind me, still grinning ear to ear. "Fucking crazy," he drawls out, sounding amused.

I blush and push my hair behind my ears. My face is hot with embarrassment. So I lost my temper. You can call me the ugliest person in the world and I will laugh in your face, but when it comes to people I care about? That is totally different.

Mary is extremely kindhearted, and that is a huge downfall but an amazing quality to have. She looks for the good in people no matter what, even when she knows better. Her cousin is a perfect example. Lexi treats her like shit, steals from her, and puts her down, but Mary keeps on caring for her.

"I need to go inside before Mary notices something." I point over my shoulder, with my thumb, toward the door. Butcher just stares at me, the corners of his mouth barely tipped up. I swear I hear him chuckle just as I close the door behind me.

"Shay! You ready?"

I scramble into the living room before Mary pops around the corner. She will never know I just handed Lexi her ass right there in her living room.

I sit down on the couch and fix my clothing before I straighten my hair. I hear Mary walking down the hallway, and

I whistle once she walks into the room. "Woah, girl! Look at you!" I catcall at her and she blushes.

She spins in a circle, completely red with embarrassment. Her long dark brown hair reaches her butt. She is around five foot seven and has curves in all the right places while rocking that doe-eyed look with her dark brown eyes.

"You ready?"

I nod and stand up. I straighten my dress and walk back to the front door. I look out the window—Butcher is sitting on his bike, staring up at the house. I am thrown back to the movie *Sixteen Candles* when Jake is waiting outside her house, leaning against his car.

"Why is he here?" Mary asks.

"He isn't bothering anyone, Mary." I give her the look, telling her to shut the fuck up about it.

I motion for her to step out first, and I follow her. She steps to the side so she can lock her door. I sneak a glance at Butcher. Much to my utter shock—but to my utter delight—he is still staring. His eyes are only on me.

Mary stops when we get to the porch steps. "Where is Lexi? She was on the couch when you showed up..." Her face is scrunched up in thought.

I suck my lips together, hoping she doesn't connect the dots. She looks back at her house and then at the ground. "I guess she just left." She shrugs.

I grab her hand and pull her in the direction of my car. "Let's forget about her. It's time for you to let loose." Mary grins.

As my hand closes around the door handle, Butcher's bike roars to life. I smile to myself.

"So he is coming to the club too?" Mary asks.

"Yeah, I guess so."

I start my car and she doesn't say a word after that. I get that it's weird, but I am not scared of it. I am not scared of him. He could have hurt me a long time ago, but he hasn't—and my brother trusts him.

She is quiet the whole way to the club, and I am getting the vibe she isn't happy with me, but I am a grown-ass woman.

When I park my car, she says, "I don't want to ruin everything. I just worry, Shay."

I give her my signature smile. "I know, Mary, but don't worry about me. I can take care of myself." I wink at her.

She bursts out laughing. "Don't I know it."

The smile drops from my face, and I frown at her in mock anger. "What is that supposed to mean?" I ask her.

She holds her stomach as she catches her breath. "Well, you do have that anger problem."

I roll my eyes, "Me? Have an anger problem?" I say in mock disbelief.

She rolls her eyes at that. "You do have an anger problem, but it's mostly for people you care about. You're just the girl who will beat somebody's ass and do it smiling."

Mary's assessment is all too accurate, and I guess it would be, because we have been friends for what seems like forever.

I shrug. "So we going to go in or what?"

As I walk toward the bar, Mary falls into step next to me. I hear a motorcycle turn off, and I realize I forgot all about Butcher following us.

We walk up to the bar and, once we are carded by the bouncer, we step inside the club. The first thing that hits me is the smell. The smell is always something you cringe over. Even though it's considered early in the nightclubbing world, the smell of body sweat and dirty sex lingers.

"Let's find a seat!" I yell into Mary's ear.

She yells back, "Okay."

We pass people who are too busy dry humping each other to know what is going on around them. We just skirt and divert ourselves from them. We spot a booth tucked into a corner. This is the perfect spot for me. It's out of the way of drunks tripping over themselves, and I like to observe.

I pull out the chair and sit down, and I set my clutch on the tabletop.

"I am going to get some drinks. You're just wanting water— am I correct?" she asks me.

I nod. "Yeah, I am driving."

She steps back through the crowd on the dance floor. I cross my legs and lean back in my seat. I look around at the people dancing. Nope, I am not looking for Butcher.

"What are you doing?"

I jump. I didn't even notice she was back. "Nothing." I grab my water and crack the lid open. A rock song comes on and I grin at Mary. She grins back and jumps out of her chair. She grabs my hand, and we walk down to the dance floor.

We grew up listening to eighties music. Our parents were obsessed, and it rubbed off on us. I throw my hands above my head and swing my hips side to side. My eyes are closed, and I am dancing to the beat. Letting loose.

"I so needed this!" Mary yells.

I open my eyes and nod in her direction. I turn around, and a man in a suit struts up to me. The closer he gets, the more I am turned off by him—by his gelled, slicked-back hair and suit that fits him perfectly. Ugh. He is too pretty! I prefer my men tattooed and badass.

All of a sudden, the guy in the suit stops walking toward me. His eyes widen, and he turns around and runs away. That is so strange, but it saves me the trouble of telling him I am not interested.

For the next thirty minutes, Mary and I rock the dance floor. We used to do this every single night, and we didn't care about drinking. We just wanted to let loose and de-stress.

College was my first taste of freedom. As the only girl in the "family," I had always been under the thumbs of my father and my "uncles" and their sons: my "cousins." That led to me being constantly protected. When I left for college...let's just say I let loose and had some fun.

I got pretty dang good at escaping my undercover bodyguards. My father and uncles thought they were slick, but I knew the moment I saw one of the guys walking across campus. They had picked a prospect at the club. How original is that? Why didn't they use someone I have never seen before?

"Lexi, what are you doing here? Who are those guys?" I spin around at the sound of Mary's voice. As she says "guys," I hear her voice crack. I take in Lexi standing there, still in my dress, and the two men behind her. This isn't good at all. I walk over to Mary and stand beside her.

"Not so tough now, are you?" Lexi sneers at me, her eyes moving up and down my body in disgust. Her lip is curled. The two men behind her laugh. Lexi turns to the side, touching one of the men on the forearm. "These men work for my boyfriend." Lexi steps away from him and toward me, her face bending toward mine like she is going to whisper something. "They are here to make you pay."

This is going to be bad. I can take out Lexi—no problem—but three at once? Yeah, the possibilities aren't going to be good. Mary gasps and scoots closer to me, and I can feel her body trembling. "What do you want to do that for, Lexi?" Mary asks, her voice quivering.

Lexi throws her head back, laughing, her fried hair not even moving. "She didn't tell you?" Lexi smiles at me menacingly.

"Tell me what?" Mary asks and I can feel her looking at me.

Lexi takes a step closer. Now I can see her two black eyes. That kind of happens when you hit someone in the nose. "Well, this bitch decided to use me as her punching bag."

I roll my eyes because she is acting all innocent and is going to make me look like the bad guy. She is the one that must bring two grown-ass men to fight me. If that doesn't scream "I am a pussy," then I don't know what does. Lexi didn't even fight me back.

"Nobody fucks with Mary," I tell her bluntly.

Lexi's eyes narrow before a slow smile slides up her pitiful face. This woman needs some serious help. She is not normal and has some major issues. I got that a long time ago, but I never expected her to bring two men to beat my ass. Those men deserve their asses beat for coming to beat up a woman. That shit doesn't fly.

"Get her, boys!" Mary screams at the top of her lungs. I brace myself for the attack. Mary grabs the back of my shirt and tries to pull me back.

Something moves in front of me, and I step aside in shock. Hands wrap around both of the men's throats.

Butcher. His face is filled with rage as he stares down at the men, his hands still wrapped around their throats, his arms flexing as he squeezes.

Butcher just saved me.

That's hot.

I hear someone gasp, and I see Lexi standing there in shock. I grin at her before looking back at Butcher, who is now staring down at me. "You got those two." I look back to Lexi and point my finger at her. "I got her."

Butcher

Shaylin grins at Lexi and takes a step closer to her. Lexi takes a step back, and Shaylin laughs before going back to smiling like a loon. Lexi starts to run away. Shaylin runs and grabs her by the hair, which she pulls with all of her might. Lexi hits the ground and wraps her hands around her hair, trying to pull it out of Shaylin's grip.

Shaylin bends down closer to her. "Why are you such a bitch!" She sighs and punches her in the face. "I." Punch. "Told." Punch. "You." Punch. "Not." Punch. "To." Punch. "Mess." Punch. "With." Punch. "ME!" She screams the last word and slams home one more punch, knocking Lexi out instantly.

That was fucking hot.

One of the men I am currently choking—his foot touches my shin. I pull them apart slightly and then slam their heads together hard. I let go of them and they slump onto the floor, knocked out.

Shaylin stands up and dusts her clothes off. She looks down at the men on the ground and grins at me.

Fucking crazy. I grin back at her. She's perfect.

Shaylin

I pull into Mary's driveway. She doesn't move and stares out the window. She hasn't said a word since everything went down. I tried talking to her many times on the way home, but she put her hand up, silencing me.

"Mary?"

She lets out a deep breath before turning to look at me. Her body is still very tense, her arms crossed across her chest and her legs crossed.

"I am moving."

My mouth falls open in shock. She is moving? "What do you mean, Mary?"

"It means exactly what I said. I am so tired of all of this!" She shakes her head.

Then it dawns on me. She wants to get away from me. I totally get it. I am not a totally normal person, nor am I sane. I fight and have a temper that gets the best of me, but I am who I am. I am the daughter of the ex-president of the Grim Sinners. I grew up seeing violence, and I wasn't affected because it happened when it was necessary.

Lexi is going to fuck with Mary and put her in a bad situation. I know it is going to happen, because it happened last time. My father got her out of that shit. Tonight, at the club, Lexi showed up with two men to beat me up. How could I let something like that go on? I could have been killed or seriously hurt. This doesn't fly with me. I don't take anything from anyone.

"You're wanting to get away from me?" I say in almost a whisper. My heart is hurting because I see Mary as a sister and I feel betrayed.

She doesn't say anything. "I just need to start fresh. I hope you understand." Mary opens my door and grabs her purse. She cranes her neck and looks back at me one more time. "Goodbye, Shay."

I turn away from her as tears roll down my face. People can throw any kind of shit at me, but the only ones who can truly hurt me are the people I love. They can hurt me the worst. I love with my whole being.

The door slams shut, and I watch as she walks into the house. I put the car in reverse and back out of the driveway.

I don't want to go home. So I go to the one person who I love more than anything in this world.

four

As soon as I drive through the gates in front of my father's house, Butcher drives away. It's been a bad night, and I just want my dad right now.

My dad is standing in the doorway. My eyes well up in tears.

Once I reach the bottom of the stairs, my dad steps out of the house. The lights come on, and I'm surrounded by the glow. "Shaylin, what are you doing here baby girl?" he booms out before he sees my face. His voice drops low and deep. "Who do I have to kill?"

I smile.

I walk up the steps and straight into his arms. I love my dad. He is this larger-than-life man who looks scary but, on the inside, he is a major softy. Well, to me he is. He is around six foot five with broad shoulders. His arms, chest, and back are covered in tattoos. His well-trimmed beard is graying, but that makes him look more handsome. "They are going to die slowly." He runs his hand down my back, which causes the tears to fall. "Very slowly." He hugs me tighter.

I laugh at this, and I lean back and dry my eyes. He grins down at me. My father is called Smiley in the MC world. He is the person who will beat your ass and do it smiling.

"Let's go in, Dad."

He narrows his eyes as he looks my face over again. He nods and presses his hand on my back, leading me into the house. I take my heels off and throw them next to the door. I loathe those things.

"Fucking hell, Shay! Why are you wearing that dress?" He slams the door shut. I laugh and walk over to the couch, where I know he keeps a throw blanket. I wrap it around my body before plopping down onto the couch.

"Dad, it isn't even short. It reaches the top of my knees." I throw this out there even though it know it's pointless.

He rolls his eyes and gives me the *look*. I smile at him and his face softens. "Shay, Shay, the only dress I want you in is an Amish dress."

At this I roll my eyes. He sits down on the couch beside me, and I know now he is done joking around. He wants to know what happened.

"What's wrong, Shay?" Dad's soft, rumbly voice washes over me, bringing comfort and security.

So I start off by telling him how I beat up Lexi at Mary's house.

My dad laughs and gives me a smile. "Well, she had it coming." He shrugs before motioning for me to continue.

I fill him in on the rest. The rest includes the two men, Lexi, and the end of my friendship with Mary. I include Butcher because he did save my butt. I twist my hands in my blanket as I watch his face reveal a million different expressions.

"They are dead," he states simply and jumps off the couch. "I got the Devils Soul enforcer to thank also. I just wish the fucker had killed them, though." My dad stops and looks at me. "Nobody dares to hurt my baby girl."

He comes back over and sits down beside me. "I will call Lane tomorrow and get this shit sorted. Mary has always been a bitch to you, sweetheart. She never accepted the MC part of you. You deserve better." Dad pulls me over to him, and I lay my head on his chest. He wraps his arm around me and kisses the top of my head. "Sleep, Smiles."

I shake with laughter at the name he gave me when I was young. Let's just say it's like father like daughter.

Butcher

My phone rings, and I reach over to my nightstand to pick it up. Tonight is the first time I have been home since I met Shaylin. She went to her father's house, and I know she is safe there. I know something went down with her friend. I could see the hurt on her face as she drove past me.

"Yeah," I say into the phone.

"It's Smiley." It's Shaylin's dad. I sit up in bed. My first thought is *something happened to Shaylin*.

"Meet me. We got some fuckers' asses to beat."

A slow smile comes over my face. Now we are talking.

"Where?"

The west side of town on Thirty-Eight. Smiley has found the fuckers who went after Shaylin. If we hadn't been in a bar, I would have ended them, but I was too busy watching Shaylin beating the chick's ass.

I climb out of bed and go to my closet, and I slip on some clothes in a hurry. I was going to find the fuckers today, but her father is already on it. They sure as fuck didn't know whose kid they were messing with, and if they only knew she was mine, they wouldn't have dared.

I walk out of my house and lock the door behind me. I hop on my bike and roar out of the driveway. Time for payback.

Smiley

I watch as Butcher parks beside me—this is the first time I have ever met this fucker. I have heard the rumors. This man is massive and fucking scarred up, and he looks mean as fuck. I already like him.

"They are at the house down the road. These fuckers do not deserve to be breathing easy," I tell him and he nods. Any man who thinks about laying a hand on a woman deserves the same kind of treatment, but tenfold.

A slow smile comes over his face. "I would have made them pay last night, but I was busy watching Shaylin beating Lexi's ass."

That's my kid. "Did she do it smiling?"

He nods and I throw my head back laughing. I watch him and I realize something. Butcher was menacing and looked evil as shit until he mentioned my baby girl's name.

Fuck me. He wants her.

"Let's roll." I start my bike and drive off in the direction of the house. He pulls up beside me. I point at the house, and we pull up in the driveway. No hiding and sneaking around. I want them to know I am coming. I want them to feel the fear.

We park and turn off the bikes. We walk side by side. Butcher steps in front of me and kicks the door off the hinges. It lands on the living room floor.

"Them." He points at two men, who scramble up off the couch when they see us.

"Well, well, well. This shit was too fucking easy." I stroll into the house and take my gun out of the holster at my back. "I've been told that you guys wanted to fuck up my daughter last night." I point my gun at them. "You messed with the wrong fucking kid."

"Do whatever the fuck you want to do with us, but keep him away." One of the men—who is the shortest and frailest—points behind me, his whole body shaking. I turn around and see Butcher running his hand up and down the side of a big-ass knife. He is staring at them with pure rage.

Hmm.

"Butcher, I think this one doesn't like you."

The pitiful fucker starts shaking so hard he falls onto the couch.

"Why did you come after my daughter?" I ask the man who is still standing.

Butcher walks behind the couch behind the man who is scared of him. He runs his knife up and down the man's cheek. The man flinches every moment.

"I was out of dope money, and the dealer said he would give me a month's supply if I roughed this chick up for him."

"Thank you." I grin and throw my fist out, nailing him on the face. He falls to the floor and I grab his shirt, lifting him off the ground. "I want you to repeat after me."

He nods frantically.

"I will never touch another female or think about it. If I do, the Grim Sinners will chop off my dick and make me eat it." I smack his mouth for good measure.

"I promise."

"Good boy, but this doesn't get you out of an ass beating. You fucked with my kid, that shit doesn't fly with me. If you touched her? You would have died a long..." I stop and bend down closer to him. "Slow, painful death."

"I am sorry!" he cries out, and I punch him in the mouth to shut him the fuck up.

"Crying and begging isn't going to do shit! You were going to hurt my kid. My..." I point to my chest. "Baby girl! The princess of the Grim Sinners. You fuckers are lucky I didn't tell her uncles and cousins. Enough chitchat. Let's get this shit started."

I grin at them before I get to work at kicking their asses. Butcher is so busy traumatizing the other guy, he won't need to have the shit kicked out of him.

I watch Butcher climb on his bike after we are done. "Treat Shay like a fucking queen or die a slow, painful death."

I leave that shit at that and climb on my bike. I drive off, leaving him there. No man is going to be good enough for my baby girl, but this one is fucking crazy enough to do whatever it takes to keep her safe.

five

A Week Later

Butcher has continued to stick around. He is outside of my house at night. I have been very tempted, many times, to just invite him in. I am a woman who lets a man make the first move. The only move Butcher has made so far is following me everywhere, and I mean everywhere. Outside of my house, work, the hair salon— hell, even when I am at my dad's house, he is outside the gate, and what shocked me more than anything was my dad waving to him.

What is up with that?

I am getting used to him following me around, and my everyday people who come in for their sweet fixes now wave at him.

I think, at this point, he just likes my cupcakes. The entire time he is in the bakery, he is stuffing his face with everything. He sits in front of the glass showcase, which can be opened from the front, so he just opens it, reaches in, and grabs whatever he wants.

Like I could tell him no.

Mary left. She left the very next day, and I can say I don't miss her. I didn't realize how negatively she affected my life. She was always a downer about the MC, who is my family. I don't think she was a bad person at all—we were friends—but she never liked a huge part of me. *Snobby* is the word for her, now that I have sat down and thought back. All I know is she moved to California. I got Lane's tech guy to track her down.

My phone starts ringing, and I look at the screen before answering. It's Chrystal, the wife of the president of the Devil Souls MC.

"Hello?" I busy myself wiping down the counter.

"Hey girl! Us and the ole ladies in the club are going to one of the club-owned male strip clubs. You in?" Chrystal sounds excited.

I look over at Butcher, who is still stuffing his face, and the moment I look at him, his head shoots around to meet my gaze. A smile comes over my face. "I am down." Butcher's eyes narrow on me.

It's time for this man to make a move and if this doesn't do it, then nothing will.

"Awesome! I will be by to pick you up at eight. Bye!" She hangs up and I set my phone down. I still feel Butcher staring at me, and I just keep on smiling.

This will be epic.

At eight o'clock on the dot, a big-ass Hummer pulls up outside my house. Butcher climbs off his bike and walks over to the Hummer. He says something and looks at the house, where I am staring out the window.

It's time for me to reveal myself. I spent two hours on this look. I open my front door and step out. I smirk and look Butcher up and down. His mouth pops open. I flip my hair over my shoulder, and I strut across my porch and down the steps, making my ass sway with every step. Butcher is standing completely still, his mouth hanging open, his fists clenched, and his body stiff. I close his mouth and drag my hand down his neck, before letting my hand fall.

The back door of the Hummer opens, and stairs pop out. I climb the stairs and plop down into the seat. I shut the door, and I am met with silence in the vehicle. I look around the Hummer, and I see everyone staring at me in awe.

"What the fuck was that?" Jean says from the back loudly.

"That, ladies, is how to hook a man." I wink at her and reach behind me to grab my seatbelt and snap it into place.

"I am in awe." I turn around and see it's Myra. When you're an MC brat, you learn who's who.

"That was pretty epic." Chrystal is still beside me.

I shrug. I am ready to end the game and see what the fuck is going on. I know one thing, and that is I am extremely attracted to him. We've been playing this game for what? Two weeks? Yeah, it's time to get where this is all leading to or to see what he wants. Him stalking me isn't the most conventional way to go about all of this but, like I said, MC men aren't normal, and Butcher is something different altogether.

"I have been dying to know what happened after he followed you out of the steak house two weeks ago," Chrystal says, and from the corner of my eye I notice all of the girls scooting closer. Hell, I even see the driver turning down the already soft radio.

"He has been stalking me," I say bluntly, and I watch a million different emotions cross their faces.

"Stalking you?" Jean says, dubious, her eyebrows furrowed.

I nod and turn in my seat slightly. A bike loudly comes up behind us, and I look out the window—it's Butcher catching up to the Hummer. "Since the moment I left the steak house, he has just been around—everywhere I go—watching me." I smile at the last part.

"Why am I not surprised? I knew the moment he followed you out, he wasn't going to leave you again." Chrystal smooths her hair over her shoulder, a bright and happy smile on her face.

"I really don't mind." I grin at all of them, and they all look at each other and smile.

"Where are we?" I ask Chrystal as we drive down a long driveway.

She looks at me as she answers. "We are here to pick up Alisha, who is an ole lady."

"Ahh," I drawl and unbuckle my seatbelt as the Hummer parks. The doors are opened and we all step out. The Hummer is more like a limo, but it is not as long. I can see that it's built for protection—I can tell the glass is bulletproof.

We all climb up the steps and onto the porch. The front of the house is literally just glass, and I've got to admit it's breathtaking. The inside is just as breathtaking.

Jean steps ahead of all of us and opens the door, and it slams against the wall. I cringe, expecting the glass door to just burst into a million pieces. We all step inside the house, and I see a small woman and a tall, muscular, tattooed man kissing.

She lets go of him and steps away, smiling at all of us. She is beautiful, and I can tell she is a couple of years younger than all of us, but not by much.

Chrystal takes her hand and then looks over at me. "This is Shaylin."

"I'm Alisha. Nice to meet you." She smiles widely at me, and she is even more breathtaking.

I smile back at her, step forward, and pull her into a hug. "Nice to meet you!" I tell her and squeeze her tighter before letting her go.

She looks at me with a sly smile on her face. "I'm guessing you're with Butcher?".

I burst out laughing because it seems like we are the talk of the town. I hold my stomach as it is already aching from laughing so much on the way over here. The other girls laugh along with me.

I wipe under my eyes. "Lane is my brother. I would have approached all of you at the restaurant, but I had to get back to work." I smile wickedly. "As for Butcher, he's been stalking my ass since then. He sleeps on my porch, he sits in my bakery all day long. He rarely talks." To confirm everything I said, I turn around and look out the window. "Like now, I bet he is at the gate waiting on me."

Everyone walks over to the window to take a look, and I join them. Butcher is sitting at the gate. Everyone bursts out laughing.

"Girl, you're in so much trouble!" Jean taunts me and cracks up.

"Come on, girls, let's go!" Myra yells, and we all file out of the house and head to the Hummer. I climb in and sit down while the others file into the other seats. It's like a bus, but it's majorly kick ass. In the main backseat are two MC prospects who weren't there before.

The Hummer starts up and we are off. We pass Butcher, who is still waiting at the gate. His eyes immediately go to me as we pass, and I smile back.

Once he is out of my line of sight, the bike starts up. My stomach flips and flutters with butterflies. A few seconds later he drives up right beside my window, and the other MC guys pull up on the other side. I look at the girls. "Told you." They all laugh, and I turn back to the window to stare at him.

"I give it two weeks before the patch is on her back!" Jean yells through the Hummer.

Alisha immediately shakes her head and holds up four fingers. "I give it four days!"

They all explode with laughter again, and I join them. Once I get myself under control, I look back out the window and wave at him. He jerks his chin in my direction and I swoon on the inside, but I totally hear the other women sigh.

A few minutes later we pull up outside the strip club, and I look out the window one last time at Butcher.

Time to get the show on the road. I grew up around badass alphas, and I know how they work.

six

One by one, we step out of the Hummer outside the strip club. I hear his bike turn off, and I grin.

"All of our men are going to die—they're going to throw a fit—but that's the fun part. It just means we get fucked into next week," Jean shrills and I shake with laughter. This girl is nuts.

All together, we walk toward the club, but I feel him coming closer and closer. I hear heavy footsteps and we all stop. Butcher thunders up to us and stands directly in front of me. He looks at the strip club sign and back at me.

"Fuck no. Mine." I am thrown over his shoulder.

Finally! This is the first time I have ever touched him, and I have wanted to so many times. Just touching him has the butterflies going crazy in my stomach. I press my hands to his back and lift myself up. I look at the girls, wink, and wave bye. My plan worked like a charm.

We move farther and farther away from the girls and into the darkness of the parking lot. Holy shit, he called me his! HOLY SHIT! He literally just claimed me.

Oh. My. God.

He bends down and I am set on my feet. I fix my hair and look up at him. I suck my bottom lip into my mouth. Now I am nervous. He bends close to me, and I suck in a deep breath. I feel something touch my back and I look around. He is holding a leather jacket.

Or maybe he was just grabbing the jacket.

Butcher is still staring at me intently when I look back at him. He lifts the jacket and opens it with both hands. I turn around and put my arms in the arm holes, and he slides the jacket on. His fingers touch the nape of my neck as he gently pulls my hair out of the jacket, and I shiver.

"Let's go," he says and I jolt at the sound of his voice again. It's so deep and manly, I want to hear it again and again. His hands touch my waist, and my hands go on top of his. He is so warm. My feet leave the ground, and he sets me on top of the motorcycle.

I lick my lips and watch as he climbs on in front of me. My heart starts pounding because I am going to be touching him and holding onto him. I shift in my seat as I scoot down toward him, but I don't put my hands around his waist.

I stare at his muscular arms as they flex with his every movement. The bike starts up, and I run my hands up and down my legs nervously.

I am so nervous because I find this man very attractive and I am a virgin. That combo is dangerous. I have dated and that's it. It never makes it past a couple of dates, and this has been going on for years. I have very high standards because, well, look at the father and uncles I have.

I know what I want in a man, and if I see this person doesn't have it, I don't continue dating him for the heck of it. If there isn't any spark, then that's it—plus I can't date a pussy. I just can't deal with a man who won't stand up for his woman or protect her.

I was on a date a year or so ago, and I was standing at the bar with him. He was ordering us a drink. Some guy came up to me and started hitting on me right in front of him.

What did my date do? He looked at the guy and turned around to get his drink. Then the guy who was hitting on me wouldn't take his eyes off of my tits, and my date noticed.

I told the guy hitting on me to hit the road, and I told my date that I was going to the bathroom when, in reality, I just left and had my brother pick me up.

Butcher reaches back and grabs my hand, and he pulls me forward so my front is pressed against his back. I lift my other hand and wrap my arms around him.

"Hold on."

You can guarantee that I will do that. I don't voice that to him though. Butcher looks from left to right and backs up with his feet. I look around the dark parking lot, and there are no people around, just a bunch of vehicles. It's a strip club with male strippers, so you can't expect a lot of men—or even women, for that matter—to be hanging around outside.

He takes off in the Texas summer. My hair moves against my skin, and I close my eyes, smiling. I love the feeling of being on the back of a bike.

I want to lay my head on his back and just snuggle up to him so flipping bad right now, but I don't have the balls to do it.

My house is just ten minutes away or so because I live close to the center of town so I can be close to my bakery.

He pulls up outside my house and drives up the driveway. That's when a million and one thoughts go through my mind at once. Is he going to come inside, or is he going to keep on sleeping outside? Maybe I should invite him in the house?

What do I do?

Once he shuts the bike off, I climb down and take off my leather jacket and helmet. I set them on the back of the bike. Butcher is studying me. My stomach flips, and I put my hands behind my back, flicking my fingers to hide my nervousness.

He climbs off his bike and I lick my lips. I start to walk to the porch, and I look back and see he is following me. Oh my goodness. My body feels like it's going to explode with nervousness. Can someone die from it?

He is so intense, and I want to ask so many questions and shake him, asking what he wants from me, but he just follows my every move. I know there is a meaning behind it—I just wish I knew what it is.

I know one thing: that I have never felt so safe in my entire life. He watches my every move, and it's like he is trying to make sure nothing happens to me. Like I said, it's intense.

I open the door, but just a crack, and I turn around expecting Butcher to be standing right behind me. No, he is sitting on the stupid lawn chair.

I turn around and walk straight into the house, bummed. "Ugh!" I mutter to myself and walk into my bedroom. I got all dressed up for nothing! He did go caveman on me and throw me over his shoulder, but he isn't doing anything else! I fully expected him to come inside the house.

I change my clothes, slipping on a pair of soft spandex sleep shorts and a soft baggy white shirt before throwing my hair into a bun. My mind is going through a hundred different things. "Grr." I walk into my bathroom to wash off my makeup and brush my teeth.

Once I am makeup free and my teeth are brushed, I come to a decision to tell him to at least come inside to sleep on my couch. I know it's not comfortable to sleep on my lawn chair every night.

I let out a deep breath and rest my forehead on the front door while pressing my hand to my racing heart. I twist the doorknob and the door opens with a creak. Butcher's head snaps up, his eyes immediately meeting mine. "Come inside? Sleep on the couch where it's comfortable at least?"

He stands up and walks toward me. I suck in a deep breath and step back into the house. He walks closer and closer to me, the light blanketing him in a soft glow.

This man is just beautiful, with all of his tattoos and his scars, his dark eyes, and his large body. He is beautiful, and now that I am looking him directly in the eyes, close up, I totally realize something.

He has pain and demons—I can see that they haunt him.

I smile at him widely. "The living room is this way." I motion for him to follow me and lead him through my dining room into my living room.

"There are blankets on the back of the couch, food in the fridge. Help yourself." I smile and point toward my room. "I am going to bed."

He doesn't say anything, just stares at me in that way he does. So I just turn around and walk into my room. I pull the door closed, but I don't shut it all the way, and I slide into my bed.

I fix the blankets all around me and turn on the TV. All I really want is to cuddle and, most of all, I am lonely. I want that companionship and the special someone that everyone else has.

My whole life I have been judged for not just dating someone to date someone, but I can't do that. I can't be with someone if I am not feeling it, especially if I don't even want to be around that person.

Closing my eyes, I sink into the pillows and blankets.

Butcher

I wait until I know she is asleep and walk to her bedroom door. The door is cracked slightly, and I push it open. She is curled up into a little ball, surrounded by blankets and pillows.

I step into her room and walk over to the edge of the bed. I stare down at her. She is beautiful. Her long blonde hair, her beautiful smile that lights up any room. She is hypnotizing.

Tonight, when I saw her heading for the strip club, I acted. I knew she was mine the moment I saw her in the steak house, but I haven't acted on it until now. Right now I want to be in this bed with her, her curled around me instead of the pillow.

She is so fucking innocent and sweet. I feel like if I touch her, I will taint her. I am not a good fucking man. I have done some horrible shit overseas that fucked with me and still fucks with me every night when I close my eyes.

I know how dangerous and sick people are in this world. I cannot bear the thought of some fucker touching her, or even looking at her. I want to rip them limb from limb and kill them over and over. She is mine and I will protect her from everything.

I saw her change before my eyes at the club the other night. She went from the sweetest little shit to a hellion in a second. She beat Lexi up and did it fucking smiling like it was just an everyday thing she does. She's got fucking crazy in her.

I like that, but she is also so fucking sweet that it hurts me. I physically ache at the sight of her, wanting to touch her. I watch her. I watch everything she does. I watch her every move, learning everything about her.

Now it's time to show her what it's like being mine.

"Good night, Shay," I whisper and take a step back, not daring to take my eyes off her.

"Goodnight, Butcher," her soft, sweet voice whispers back.

I turn around and force myself out of the room.

seven

Shaylin

Waking up the next morning, I turn over to look at the clock, which says 8:00 a.m. Yawning, I throw my arms above my head and stretch. That's when it hits me.

Butcher is in my living room.

I tiptoe to my door and peer into the living room. He is still lying on the couch, stretched out, asleep. I will make us some breakfast before I head to work.

He was in my room last night. I pretended to sleep as he watched me. When he whispered goodnight to me, my heart skipped a beat. I want to say so much to him, but I don't know what to say first.

I shuffle sleepily into the kitchen and pull out a pack of bacon and some eggs from the refrigerator. Then I put the bacon on the stove because it takes longer to fry.

Thirty minutes later breakfast is ready and he hasn't come into the kitchen. I was sure he would appear once he smelled bacon. I sit down and eat my food, and he doesn't come in.

After putting my dishes in the sink, I peek into the living room. He is still fast asleep on his side, facing the couch.

Now I feel bad—I guess sleeping outside in my lawn chair for the last week or so hasn't been very comfortable. He must be exhausted.

As I get dressed, I look at the clock. I've got fifteen minutes to get ready. I slide on my work clothes and throw my hair up in a bun before putting on some mascara and foundation. I grab my purse off my vanity chair before walking out of my bedroom. His food will get cold, so I will set it on the stove and leave him a note to lock up when he leaves.

I shut the door quietly behind me and unlock my car as I walk down the path, and I take one last look at my house.

I like the idea of him being here.

Butcher

I wake suddenly and look around the room, and it hits me that I am still at Shaylin's. I take my phone out of my pocket. I see it's ten o'clock in the morning. She has already left for work.

Panic hits me like a freight train. The thought of something happening to her and my not being there to protect her is staggering. Nothing can happen to her. It just can't.

I can't explain why I feel so fiercely protective of her. I lost my family the moment they were out of my sight, and that fucked with me. The way she smiles at fucking everyone and is so trusting—her innocence makes me want to protect that part of her.

I need to see her.

I run out of the house, but I make sure to lock the door before taking off toward my bike with only one thought on my mind.

Get to her.

Shaylin

The door to the bakery slams open and my head flies up, my eyes wide in shock. Butcher is standing at the entrance looking

55

around the room frantically. His body is visibly shaking. I run out from behind the counter.

Butcher's eyes snap to mine, and he relaxes slightly before he stalks over to me. My breath comes out in whooshes, as my heart is pounding out of my chest and my body is tense.

He stops right in front of me and I stand completely still, not daring to take my eyes from his. His hand shoots out suddenly and hooks around the back of my neck. I gasp at the feel of him touching me.

"What's the matter?" I get out before I am slammed against his chest. My hands shoot out to his sides in utter shock. Did something happen? Butcher bends down and tightens his arms around me. I hear him inhale, and shivers move up my back.

"Butcher?" I whisper against his large chest, my hands fisted in the back of his shirt. He doesn't say anything, but he does continue to hug me. I am so confused, but I feel like something major just happened.

One of his hands drags up my back to the back of my neck before slipping into my hair, allowing me to move from the position I am in. So I just let him hold me, and I've got to admit I love the feeling of being held like this.

I close my eyes and move closer to him, if that is even possible, sinking into the hug. I breathe in his warm and woodsy scent.

"Shay," he breathes against my neck, and I run my hands up his muscular back.

"Yeah?" I whisper back.

"You're mine."

My eyes open and I lean back to look at him. His hand isn't in my hair anymore. "I am yours?" I repeat, but this time I am looking him directly in the face, and his expression is tender.

His hand comes up to my face, cupping my jaw. "Yes."

I swallow my emotions and smile at him widely. "Okay," I whisper and he gives me a small smile—it's not much, but it is something.

The bell on the door chimes, and the moment is broken. I take a step back and smooth the flyaways around my face. I look over Butcher's shoulder, and I see one of my regulars standing there.

"I've got to get back to work."

He nods. I go back behind the counter, and he moves over to his regular seat in the corner. My mind is reeling at what just happened. He just told me flat out that I was his, and I agreed. I agreed! That shit is a serious thing in the MC world. I know one thing: I like him a lot.

The day passes by in a blur. At one point, Butcher left for an hour, but otherwise he has never been far from my side. He even follows me into my house after work.

"I am going to change!" I yell over my shoulder and walk into my bedroom. I stop once I see what is on my bed: the dress that went missing off the back of the door at the shop when I took my niece out.

He stole my dress. I burst out laughing and fall onto the bed, clutching my stomach. I can't believe he did this! He took this dress off the back of the door, and then he hid the whole rack! That makes me laugh even harder. You've got to give him props for that one. I believe he could write the alpha male handbook.

I spend the next hour getting ready, taking the time to curl my long blonde hair into loose waves. I stand in front of the wall-length mirror. The dress isn't too short, and it compliments my curvy figure.

Tonight I am braving heels—I guess I want to bring myself a bit closer to Butcher's height. That man is hitting six foot four or five, and I'm just five three with shoes on! The shoes matter when you are short. The heels are four inches high, and I know I will be crawling by the end of the night if I don't break a bone.

I used to be the world's clumsiest person. My dad threatened daily to wrap me in bubble wrap because I tripped over everything. I tripped going up stairs—who else can do that? I fell walking on a flat surface. I was just doomed. Luckily, when I got older, I grew out of it, but some days it catches back up with me when I least expect it.

Taking one last long look at myself, I walk over to my bedroom door and put my hand on the doorknob. I suck in a deep breath to control the butterflies in my stomach. It's like my skin is hyperaware.

I twist the handle and step out, my head held high. I look into the living room, and Butcher is standing in front of my couch staring directly at me. I let out a deep breath and smile at him. Butcher's eyes leave mine and look up and down my body, leaving a trail of fire in its wake.

He takes a step in my direction, and I freeze. With every step my heart pounds harder until I can feel it in my throat.

He stops in front of me and looks down at me. I lick my dry lips and smile slightly. My hands run up and down my hips to control my nervousness. I am a confident person, but Butcher just puts me on edge and brings out the giddy teenage feelings out of nowhere.

His hand moves toward my face, and he touches a piece of my hair. His fingers run down the length of it before moving back to my face, and he tucks the piece of hair behind my ear, his fingers just barely brushing my cheek.

"Beautiful."

My heart stops right there, and I feel like I could fall onto the floor in a pile of goo. I have been called beautiful many times, but coming from Butcher it's totally different. For the first time in my life, every insecurity is gone.

I touch his hand, which is still resting on my ear and cheek. "Thank you, but you're beautiful too." I watch his face shift in confusion, which causes me to laugh.

Butcher is beautiful in his own right. He is not beautiful in the conventional sense of word. He is too masculine. But he is beautiful in the way he carries himself, the way he protects the people he cares about, and the scars that riddle his body. A scar on the upper cheekbone on the right side of his face stands out the most. But I can't see most of his scars very well because of his tattoos.

To show him what I mean, I touch the scar. "Beautiful," I whisper.

"Shay," he growls and takes my hand from his face. My eyes widen, and my wrist is wrapped around his hand. The hand that was touching my cheek snakes around the back of my head, holding me completely still.

His face leans down toward mine, and my breathing grows rapid at the thought of him kissing me, but he doesn't.

He kisses my forehead.

Closing my eyes I sink into the kiss. This isn't just a kiss on the forehead. A forehead kiss can mean many things: respect, protection, adoration. I breathe in his woodsy scent, and my thoughts are on one thing right now.

He is mine.

eight

Butcher is taking me to one of the fancier restaurants in town, so we aren't on his bike. We are in a huge black truck that I needed help climbing into. I don't think I have any dignity left after trying to bring my leg up to step into the vehicle on top of wearing heels. It wasn't a great time.

Walking into the restaurant, we are met by a waitress. "Name?"

"Dean."

I look at Butcher in shock—his name is Dean? I can't see him being anything other than Butcher. The man looks like a butcher, if you know what I mean, but road names are there for a reason in the MC. I can only guess where he got the name Butcher.

"Follow me," the waitress says, wide eyed, looking at Butcher.

I laugh under my breath at the sight of her face. She picks up two menus and heads toward the back of the restaurant. As we follow her, Butcher's hand rests on the small of my back. Everyone turns to look at us as we pass, and Butcher stares every single one of them down, especially the men. He radiates safety and protection—it oozes out of him. The way his hand touches the small of my back, his body slightly curled into my mine to block me from harm, and the way he watches everyone in the room.

"Here you are!" the lady seating us exclaims loudly with a smile way too big.

"Thank you." I smile and sit with my back to the room, and Butcher visibly relaxes. He sits down in front of me, looking massive and imposing.

The hostess walks away, practically running. I get it: the man is scary, but at least try to hide it. I turn back around to face Butcher, who is staring at me. I smile and look down before grabbing the menu resting in front of me.

"What can I get you guys to drink?" A loud voice directly beside me asks and I jump, my hand flying to my chest. Butcher growls, and I look over and see a waitress standing there with a notepad in her hand. "I am sorry for scaring you."

I wave my hand in front of me before flashing her a quick smile. "It's no biggie. I will take a glass of white wine."

She writes it down and then looks at Butcher.

"Bud Light."

She grimaces and writes down his drink order. I do a mental eye roll. "I will go get your drinks." She walks away.

"Where are you from?" I ask Butcher and smile slightly.

"Tennessee." He sits back in his seat, relaxing.

I gnaw on my bottom lip because I want to know so much about him. "What brought you to Texas?" I fiddle with the edge of the menu.

Butcher's eyes search my face and then look down at my hands. I feel like he can sense my nervousness. "I wanted a fresh start."

That I get. I look down and mess with the napkin on my lap. "Ah, I see."

"Smile."

My head shoots up at his abrupt tone. Butcher leans toward me. "What?" I say breathlessly, tucking a piece of hair behind my ear.

"Smile, never stop smiling, and don't be nervous around me. Never around me."

My heart stops at his words, and a huge smile breaks out across my face. I never imagined he could be sweet. His face softens at the sight, and his hand comes up to my jaw, his thumb brushing the side of my mouth. "That's better."

Dude, my stomach flips over. "Did anyone ever tell you that you are a sweetheart?"

His eyes open wide in surprise. "I'm not sweet," he grumbles and sits back in his seat, fixing a glare on me.

Oh yeah, Butcher, I got your number. I arch my eyebrow at him. "Maybe not to everyone else, but you are to me." I smirk at him and stand up. "I will be back, order for me if she comes back. I need to go to the ladies room."

At that I step away from the table and cross the room, leaving him with his thoughts. We are in one of the rooms that people can rent, and it's kind of secluded. We are the only customers besides a group of men sitting a few booths down.

A piece of paper falls off the men's table and hits the ground in front of me. I know they just wanted to see me bend down, so I bend at the knees and squat down, not giving them the satisfaction. I grab the piece of paper and set it down on the table, looking at the man who dropped it. "I don't fall for shit like that, grow the fuck up."

His mouth pops open, and he looks me up and down. "Baby, I could have you bent over this table in a few seconds flat."

"Sure, that would be the day, asshole, keep telling yourself that." I laugh out loud and walk past them. That guy is a total fool. Every single one of those men has "douche bag" written all over him—with their all-too-pretty-boy looks. Pussies—all of them.

Butcher

"I could have you bent over this table in a few seconds flat."

Rage hits me hard and fast. I stand up and stalk over to the men, making sure Shaylin goes into the bathroom before I approach them. I spot a steak knife on an empty table and grip it in my hand. The man's hand is resting on the table on top of the note Shaylin picked up off the floor.

Nobody fucking disrespects her like that. Ever. That shit doesn't fucking happen and sure as fuck doesn't happen in front of me.

I slam the knife into the table between his fingers, making sure to catch the skin where his fingers meet. The fucker brings his hand back, crying out in pain.

I roll my eyes at the pussy. His head shoots around, and he looks at me. He and his buddies take me in. *Fucking take me in. I'm your fucking nightmare.*

"What's up, man?" the one who dropped the note and disrespected my woman blubbers.

"You said you could bend my woman over the table in ten seconds flat?"

He and the other fuckers pale. "Man, I didn't know she was with someone," he stammers, and that makes me even more mad. Who gives a fuck if she was with me or not—that doesn't give him the right to speak to anyone like that.

That pisses me off.

I grip him by the throat and lift him out of the booth. He stands up next to me, his hands on my wrists. I let go of his throat and he starts to back away, but I place my hand on the back of his neck.

"What are you doing?" he asks.

But those are the only words he is getting the fuck out. I slam his face into the table, and I hear the satisfying sound of his nose breaking. "Now who is bent over the fucking table in ten seconds?" I chuckle and press his face harder into the table before letting go.

He stands up and grabs his nose before sitting down, and his buddies immediately start fussing over him.

I go back to the table just as the waitress arrives. "The lady will have a honey-glazed salmon topped with citrus avocado salsa, and I will have the eight-ounce steak topped with seared scallops."

I hand her both of the menus, and she thanks me and leaves.

"What did I miss?" Shaylin asks and sits down in the chair in front of me.

"Nothing, I just ordered the food." I wink and sit back in my chair.

She smirks at me like she knows more than I think she does. "Sure you did." At that I flat out grin. I'm busted.

Shaylin

As I leave the bathroom, my eyes go to the man I called out, and he is sitting there holding his nose. He sees me walking toward him, and he almost crawls under the table.

Butcher.

Butcher must have heard what he said to me. I laugh under my breath and return to my table. "What did I miss?" I can't resist asking.

"Nothing, I just ordered the food." He winks and gives me a smug look.

I give him a sly grin, letting him know that I know that's far from the truth. "Sure you did," I say sarcastically and he flat out grins.

I suck in a sharp breath. Fuck, he is beautiful and dangerous. It should be a crime for someone to look like that.

According to the MC grapevine, Butcher serves in the Navy SEALs. "Did you always want to be a SEAL?"

He nods and takes a sip of his beer. "You always want to bake?"

I laugh and nod. "Yeah, I have loved it for as long as I can remember. I used to stand in a chair to reach the top of the counter to stir all of my ingredients together. It was horrible, but my dad and uncles pretended it was the best thing ever."

Butcher smiles at me, his eyes lit up. "I like your baking."

I laugh again and sling my hair over my shoulder. "I noticed that, you've demolished at least a dozen cupcakes a day since you met me."

He shrugs. "Damn good."

I nod. "Yeah, because I made them."

His shoulders shake with laughter, and I smile wide. I want him to laugh more often. A figure rushes past us, practically running, and I turn around to see who it is. It's the man whose nose Butcher busted. He keeps glancing back at Butcher, and Butcher drags his steak knife across his throat. That's all it takes for me to burst out laughing. Butcher drops the steak knife, and it hits the top of the table. That was epic—he's fucking crazy.

The waitress comes back with our food. "Here you are." I wipe under my eyes to get rid of the tears and sit back in my chair so she can set my food on the table. I look at what he ordered, and it's one of my favorite meals. He is staring at me, gauging my reaction. "This is perfect. Thank you."

He looks down and starts cutting into his steak. I grab my silverware and get busy putting away my own food. I am not ashamed to admit that I ate every bit of what was on my plate.

Once we are finished eating, he pays for the food and we walk, side by side, through the restaurant, his hand on my hip this time. I lick my parched lips and take in deep breaths to contain myself. I like that he is touching me now and he did it without thinking twice.

"Shaylin?"

I turn around and see one of the guys I went on one date with. Butcher's hand tightens on my hip possessively. I wave to the guy and turn away. We went on one date—what did he expect?

"Too many dicks in here," Butcher growls. I grin and wrap my arm around his back.

"Let's go then." I lay the back of my head against his chest, looking up at him. Butcher's glare drops as he looks down at me.

We walk out of the restaurant and into the darkness of the parking lot. Butcher pulls me tighter into him, like he is shielding me with his body.

When he opens the door of his truck, I grab the oh-shit handle and lift my leg inside. Hands wrap around my hips, and I am lifted into the truck.

"Thank you." I wink at him and he shakes his head at me. When he backs out of the parking lot, I put on my seatbelt and take off my heels, which are hurting my feet.

He offers me his large tattooed hand and twines his fingers through mine. He lays our joined hands in his lap, and I turn away, hiding my goofy smile.

"Feet hurt?"

"Yeah, I hate heels." I smooth my hair over one shoulder.

"You're just as beautiful without them."

My jaw hits the floor again. This man is seriously sweet. "Sweet," I say simply and he shakes his head again.

"Speaking the truth."

He pulls onto my street.

"Still sweet," I drawl.

"It's not sweet when you're being honest."

I point at him. "See! Sweet!" I say it loudly this time, and he shakes his head again. I don't say anything else because he is going to disagree, but we both know the truth here. The truth is he is sweet to me, but we got a visual of how unsweet he was earlier.

After he pulls into my driveway, without a word, he lifts me out of the truck, holding me bridal style.

"What are you doing?"

He shuts the door and carries me up the walkway to my porch. "Your feet hurt."

And he says he isn't sweet.

nine

Shaylin

We walk inside my house, and he sets me down on the floor. If he were really worried about my feet, he wouldn't have set me down so soon. I do believe he just wanted to carry me.

"I am going to change into something comfortable." I walk into my bedroom, leaving Butcher in the living room. I am assuming he is going to go change too, since he carried a bag in earlier.

I change into a pair of sweatpants and another baggy shirt that hangs off my shoulder. I throw my hair into a bun and make quick work of ridding myself of my makeup.

About ten minutes later, I walk into my living room. Butcher is sitting back on my couch, shirtless and in a pair of sweats. Those abs and tattoos! Sweet baby Jesus, give me strength. I feel my face getting hot—I know I am red with embarrassment.

Growing a set I sit down on the couch. I sit a foot away from him, but what I really want is to be pressed against that hard chest. "What do you want to watch?" I ask hesitantly then switch on the TV.

"Get your ass over here."

I drop the remote and pick it up. "What?" I ask and set the remote on the coffee table in front of us.

"Over here."

I scoot over to him, and I slowly lie down with my head on his chest. The moment I touch his bare chest, I swoon to myself. I've got to save some dignity. This is what heaven is.

His arm comes off the back of the couch and rests on my back with his hand on my hip. Not able to help myself, I bring my hand up his belly, slowly dragging it to his chest.

I feel him shiver, and I cover my mouth so I don't make a sound. I like that he is affected by me like I am by him.

A few minutes into the TV show, he starts to move his hand up and down my back, which is a major weakness of mine. Eventually his hand snakes beneath my shirt to rub my back, his fingernails gliding down my back.

"Are you trying to make me go to sleep?" I sigh and burrow my head deeper into his chest. With my free hand, I grab my hair tie, letting my hair fall around me.

His hand sinks into my hair, and he lets his nails drag across my skin. I think I am going to marry him after this. "If you keep on doing that, I am going to fall in love with you." I yawn again.

"That's the plan."

I freeze and blink a few times. Did he just say that or did I imagine it? To confirm, I climb off of him and onto my knees facing him.

"Did you just say that?" I ask in a whisper.

He nods and smiles. I lean forward, wrapping my arms around his neck, hugging him. My cheek lands against his, and I breathe in his intoxicating scent, which is all male. He moves his cheek from mine, and then those lips touch my forehead.

I sit perfectly still, letting him do whatever he wants. I keep my eyes closed. His lips leave my face, and my stomach clenches in anticipation of what will happen next.

His lips touch my cheek, and I jump slightly at the contact. I rest my hands on his shoulders.

His lips touch the corner of my mouth and I scoot closer, wanting them to move that small distance to my lips.

Then it happens. His lips touch mine, and the moment they do it feels like I have been electrocuted. I gasp and bring my hands to the back of his head, and I twine my fingers through his hair.

Butcher growls and grabs my hips, pulling me fully into his lap, my legs on either side of him. His large hand moves up my back and then into my hair, taking complete control of the kiss.

His lips move over mine and I open my mouth, sinking into the kiss. I bring one hand from his hair to his jawbone. I feel his jaw move with his movement on my lips. I shudder and bring my body closer to him. Chest to chest.

His hand sinks into my hair, and he kisses me back harder. He takes my lip into his mouth, and I open my eyes. He drags his teeth across my bottom lip. "Mine," he growls loudly, his eyes dark. His hand falls to my ass and—with both hands—he squeezes, pulling me harder against him.

That's when I notice how hard he is, and it's instinctual to rock my hips. That movement has me shuddering with pleasure. I fall forward, bringing my lips back to his, and I move my hips again, moaning against his mouth. He kisses me and pulls me harder against him.

I want him so bad, I feel like I am burning from the inside out. He stands and I wrap my legs around his waist. As he walks toward the bedroom, I don't take my mouth from his.

A second later I feel my bed at my back, and I sink into the mattress. I don't unhook my legs from Butcher. I feel his arms on either side of my head, and his body is pressed against mine.

He touches my hip and I moan. It's so close.

His mouth breaks from mine, and he looks into my eyes. "What do you want?"

My chest is moving rapidly because I am out of breath. "I don't know," I tell him honestly. "I've never been with a man before, I haven't ever been touched by one before," I whisper to him, almost ashamed. What twenty-five-year-old girl has never been with a man before?

Butcher's face changes, and a large smile comes over his face—it's utterly breathtaking. I bring my hand up and cup his jaw.

He smiles wider and looks down at my lips, then at my eyes. I feel his hand move from my hip to my pussy, and it cups me. I jolt at the feel of him touching me, a thrill shooting through my body.

"Arms above your head."

I shiver with excitement and nervousness. I sit up and he sits next to me. I raise my arms above my head. He yanks off my shirt and takes in the sight of me in my bra. He pulls my pants down my legs and throws them across the room.

I lie back down on the bed, and I scoot back so my head is lying on my pillow.

Butcher moves back to me, placing his body on top of mine and his face directly above mine. "I will not fuck you today," he says in his deep, rough voice. His lips kiss mine softly then gradually move to my neck. I arch my neck, giving him better access, and goose bumps break out across my skin.

"Today."

I open my eyes and look at him. He slides his hand behind my back. I feel my bra coming loose, and he lifts it off my arms. He throws it on the floor and gives me a wicked smile that tells me I am going to enjoy every second of this.

His hand closes around the waistband of my panties, and I clench in anticipation. I lick my lips, wondering what he's going to do next. "Today..." He tightens his grip on my panties. "Today, I fucking taste every single part of your body, learning what makes you squirm, what makes you yell my name, and what makes you come over and over." He rips the panties from my body, and they land on the ground.

Oh my god. Fuck me. I am completely naked in front of him right now. The only times I have been naked is when I am getting waxed or with my doctor.

My eager eyes follow his every move. He takes in my body, going from my feet to the top of my head. It takes everything in me not to cover myself. I am not self-conscious—it's just instinctual.

"You're gorgeous."

I melt right there and then, and his face leaves my body and he looks deeply into my eyes.

"You're the most beautiful woman I have ever seen."

"Butcher," I whisper and sit up and press my lips to his. He is just perfect. He breaks the kiss and presses his forehead against mine, and I see him grin. "Now the fun begins."

He scoots down my body, his lips moving to my shoulders. He kisses them and moves to the dip in my neck. He dips his tongue in, and I jerk at the feel. My hands go the back of his head, sinking into his hair.

His mouth moves between my breasts, kissing and licking. Torture—I believe that is what you can call this.

I take one hand from his hair and drag it down his back, my nails scouring it slightly. I feel his breath on my nipples for a split second before his mouth closes around the left nipple. Pleasure shoots straight down to my pussy. I cry out, and my hand goes back to his hair and instinctively pulls it.

He chuckles and moves on to the other nipple, and I throw my head back. I pull his hair again. I can't help it. It gets intense for a split second, and it just happens for the next minute or so, dragging out my torture. I will take this torture any day though.

His lips leave my breasts and move down to my stomach, closer and closer to my...

Holy shit! Is he going to do what I think he is?

My question is answered shortly as he slides off the end of the bed and lands on his knees. His hands wrap around my knees, and I am pulled to the edge of the bed. I laugh at the sudden movement. He takes my knees and lifts them over my shoulders, leaving him facing me there.

I raise my head and look down at him wide eyed. He smirks at me and then lowers his head. Oh shit. "AHH!" I yell out. His tongue flicks my clit and it's fucking intense. He does this over and over again.

My head is thrown back, my back slightly arched, and my hands buried deep in my covers. "Butcher," I grunt and run my toes down his bare back. I am so close, so close, but I just need something.

He slides a finger inside of me and curls his finger.

I shatter into a million pieces. My body tightens up, and I feel my pussy pulsating around his finger. My shoulder jerks at the power of the orgasm, and I dig my head into the blanket beside my head, biting it, as I come down from the earth-shattering orgasm I just had.

Arms wrap around me, and I am lifted off the bed. I let go of the blanket and look up at Butcher, who has a smug smile on his face. I laugh softly to myself and lay my hand on his warm chest.

I am laid down on the bed, my head on the pillow, and Butcher walks to the light switch and turns it off. When he gets in bed, I'm still lying on my back, and I bring the blanket up to cover us up.

Butcher scoots over until we are touching. He kisses me on the cheek and lowers his head into my neck. His arm comes up and wraps around my neck, his palm resting on the pillow beside my head, and his body covers mine. I look to the bedroom door and then at Butcher.

"Butcher," I say softly and he mutters, "Hmm."

"You're covering my body with yours, you're protecting me. That's why you slept outside my house. You're protecting me," I whisper and move closer to him, kissing the top of his head.

He moves his hand from my pillow to my cheek. "It kills me to think of something happening to you."

I clamp my eyes shut to hold back tears. I have been protected my whole life, but for someone to go to such lengths to make sure nothing hurts me—I can't describe the emotions I am feeling.

"Goodnight," I whisper, my eyes still closed.

"Goodnight, Shay." He takes his hand from my face, and I fall asleep smiling.

ten

I woke up late for work, and that means the shop didn't open until an hour past the time it was supposed to. I ran around like a chicken with its head cut off, slipped on some clothes, and ran out the door with Butcher hot on my heels.

Last night was just crazy, and I can't believe everything that happened. I blushed all morning thinking about what went down—and Butcher went down. Ha, get it? Don't get me wrong—I have come before, but it's a lot different when someone else is doing it to you.

Butcher parks his bike and walks across the street to get breakfast.

Luckily, I had everything prepped last night or I would be really hurting. I need to hire on some full-time staff. The past year the bakery has grown beyond what I could imagine.

The buzzer in the kitchen goes off, letting me know my batches of cupcakes are finished. I walk into the kitchen and open my many ovens. I grab my rolling table and the oven mitts hanging on the wall.

After putting the mitts on, I reach inside the oven. In each hand I take a tray of cupcakes out, and I set them on the table.

I hear the bell above my door ding, and I turn off the oven. I will come back for the rest. When I get halfway across the kitchen, I hear a loud crash. I freeze and my heart stops, expecting the worst.

I look up at the security monitor, and I see three men. They have bandanas over their faces and guns. One of the men is behind the counter. I hear the loud crash again, and I see him banging on the register.

Fuck fuck fuck. Butcher is across the street, and I don't have his number. Taking out my phone, I step back from the doorway, my heart pounding so hard I feel like they can hear it. I put the phone on silent and send a text to my father. He will know Butcher's number.

ME: Dad, three people have broken into the bakery. I am in the back and they don't know I am here. Butcher is across the street to get breakfast.

I hit send and stuff my phone back in my pocket. Then it hits me that I have a gun stored under this cabinet. I get on my hands and knees, reach under the cabinet, and grab the gun.

I check to see how much ammunition I have and see I have a full clip. I push the clip back in, cock the gun, and take off the safety. I am not taking chances. I stand back, put my back to the corner, and ready myself.

"Wait," a voice says and I stiffen. "Someone has to be here, the store wouldn't be open."

Fuck me!

I bite my bottom lip, making sure I stay silent. There is literally nowhere to hide in my kitchen. I wanted a huge open floor plant. Big mistake, obviously. A figure moves in front of the entrance to the kitchen, and he walks inside. "Well, look what we have here!"

I have the gun hidden behind my back. "Take the money and go." I don't want this to end badly.

"We can't leave a witness. Sorry, puss." I see a marking on the side of his neck. He raises the gun. He is going to kill me.

"You don't have to do this." I try to keep my voice even and steady, not wanting to give in to my fear. The fear is gut wrenching. It's three against one and they are armed. Why are they robbing a bakery in the middle of the day?

He steps forward and brings the bandana from his mouth. He sneers at me, and I notice the tattoo on the side of his neck. I know it's related to some kind of gang or group. That's not fucking good.

"We can set up an arrangement to get you out of it." His eyes move up and down my body. Vomit moves up my throat. This is sickening and it pisses me off.

It's like something comes over my body when I am pissed. Fear is gone out the window. "No arrangement." I am getting madder every second. His eyes are lingering on my tits.

He laughs and his eyes move from my tits to my face. "Nah, I don't need an arrangement. I am just going to take it, whether you want it or not."

Fuck that shit.

I grin at him, showing teeth and all. "Big mistake."

I bring my gun out from behind my back, point it at his crotch, and pull the trigger. He falls to the ground screaming. I run over and kick the gun out of his hand, and it skids across the floor. "Now you ain't going to be doing shit." I kick him in the face, knocking him out cold.

Adrenaline is pumping through me, and I hear someone running in my direction. I ready myself. A gunshot goes off and then another. A man falls into the kitchen. He lands head first, blood immediately pooling around him.

"SHAYLIN!" Butcher roars and I jump into action.

"I'm okay!" I yell. I hear thundering footsteps, and he charges into the room. He looks at the man I shot in the crotch, before running over and swooping me up in his arms.

"Don't fucking do that shit again."

I wrap my arms around him tighter, my body shaking with emotion. I hear someone moaning, and I feel Butcher stiffen before he lets me go. He shields me with his body. I peek around his side. The man I shot in the crotch is awake and moaning, holding himself.

"Why did you shoot him in the crotch?" Butcher says in an eerily cool and collected voice.

"He threatened to rape me."

My body gets a jolt as I say the word "rape. "It hits me what just came down: I could have been raped. This could have been a very bad situation. Lucky I had a gun and Butcher was here.

"Dead man, but not yet." I can hear the smile in his voice. Butcher walks over to the cabinet, grabs a towel, and throws it to him. "It's not your time yet."

Chills run up my spine at the sound of his voice. This man isn't going to die easy. I feel my phone vibrating in my pocket and, with a very shaky hand, I bring it out. I look at the screen and see it's my father.

"He-hel-hello," I choke out as the adrenaline is wearing off and everything is starting to sink in.

"Shay, are you okay? What happened?" Dad's words rush out, and I hear a bunch of motorcycles in the background. I feel someone standing in front of me, and I look up. Butcher has his hand out to take the phone from me.

"Butcher here." I hear my father in the background, speaking a mile a minute. I rush into Butcher's arms. I just need to feel safe right now. I am a tough girl and I don't take shit from anyone, but this has rocked me to my core. I never expected this to happen.

I hear a bunch of motorcycles pull up outside, and Butcher ends the phone call with my dad and stuffs it in my back pocket. Butcher holds me tightly to him, my face buried in his chest.

"You are never leaving my sight again." He squeezes me tighter to him.

"I don't want to," I admit and fist the back of his cut. Even after this happened, I feel safe right now. I feel safe wrapped up in his arms. This is a freak thing that happened, but one of the risks of having your own store is that someone might try to rob you.

It could have been a lot worse.

"Butcher!"

I look up at the entrance to the kitchen and see a bunch of Devil Souls members walk through that door: Kyle, Ryan, Torch, Techy, Vinny, Jack, Trey, and Locke.

"What the fuck happened?" Kyle asks and takes a step forward.

"Someone tried to rob me." I feel a lot better now, and I can hear it in my voice. I tighten my grip on Butcher and move away slightly, but his hand on my back presses me against him tighter than before. I guess I am not moving.

"We will get this shit cleaned up. Smiley on his way?" Kyle asks and whistles as he takes in the guy sitting up against the wall holding a towel to his crotch. Kyle's body stiffens and he looks at me. "This your work?"

I nod. "He said some offensive things."

Kyle grins and then looks at the other members. "We will be having some fun later, boy, and wait till you meet her dad."

I grin at that.

We hear a roar of motorcycles outside, and I look up at Butcher. He kisses my forehead, and I close my eyes, letting the feeling of safety and everything Butcher wash over me.

I hear my door open and the sound of a lot of footsteps. I guess the uncles came too. First my father is through the door, then Lane, and then everyone else. Butcher stiffens and takes a step back like he is ready to run off with me, hiding me from everyone.

My father couldn't give two fucks, though. He plucks me out of Butcher's arms and into his. "I have never been so fucking scared in my life. Don't do that shit again." I laugh slightly at that because Butcher said the same thing. Butcher may have let my father have me, but he is still touching me.

"Dad, my turn." Lane steals me from my dad, and I feel Butcher moving with me. One by one, I am passed around to all twenty people.

"What the fuck happened, Shay?" My father asks once I am free of everyone. Butcher backs away from everyone, tucking me close to his body, and he ignores all the glares he is getting from the members of Lane's club.

"I was here in the back, and I heard a loud crash." I go into full detail, even repeating exactly what the man said to me. The culprit is very much alive and is staring at everyone wide eyed, looking terrified.

I can't feel sorry for someone when earlier he threatened to kill me and do awful stuff to me. I am getting mad again thinking about it.

Smiley and Lane step forward at the same time, but my father is the only one who smiles like it's the best day on Earth. "Big mistake," Dad says. The guy looks like he is going to piss himself, but I am not sure he can do that anymore, considering. Smiley looks down at the blood and then at me, grinning. "You blew his dick off." He turns back to the man. "Did she do it smiling?"

My mouth pops open, and I stare at my father in shock. Did he just ask that? The guy nods and pales further.

Dad grins at everyone and says, "That's my baby girl."

There is no hope of escaping from my dad. I wrap my arms around Butcher and lay my head on his chest, feeling exhausted all of a sudden.

"I'm taking her home. I will be at the club later for some fun." Butcher growls at the last part, and everyone in the room nods. Butcher practically carries me through the back door.

Butcher

The phone call that fucking changed my life. Her father called me, and it only took the sound of her name coming out of his mouth to spring me into action. I ran across the parking lot and crossed the street in what seemed like hours but was only a few seconds. I heard a gunshot just as I stepped on the sidewalk. I threw the door open, took my gun out, and shot the fucker who was heading for the back and then the other, who was standing behind the counter. I yelled her name, and when she answered I almost fell to the fucking ground in relief.

I run into the kitchen, and she seems like she is perfectly fine. I look at the man lying on the ground, a few feet away from her, out cold. I split the distance from her and wrap her in my arms. I breathe in her scent and touch her all over to make sure she isn't hurt and to remind myself she is still here.

Rage is something I have become accustomed to, but it's nothing compared to my rage over something happening to her. I am going to track down every single person who had a part in this and rip them apart.

Someone moans, and I look around to see the man with a shot to the dick.

I ask her why she did it, and I know the reason before she even tells me.

I look at the man and mouth to him, "Dead man." He pales and I grin at him. This is going to be fucking fun.

Shaylin

I just want to go home and curl up in bed, binge watching TV. Today has been awful. Never once did I think I would be robbed in the middle of the day. I just can't wrap my head around it or the fact that I shot him in the dick. I do believe he deserved that, though.

Butcher is half carrying me out of the store as he takes me to his motorcycle. I feel him looking at me, and I know he is concerned. I will be fine. I just want to get away from all of the bodies.

Most of all I just want Butcher to hold me.

We reach his bike. He puts the leather jacket on me, and I look up at him. His eyes are searching my face, and I give him a small smile. Butcher's whole body relaxes, and he touches the side of my face. "There's my Shay."

That brings a full grin to my face, and I fall into his arms. I close my eyes, as my head lands on his warm chest, and breathe in his scent. His lips touch the top of my head, and I twist my hands in the back of his shirt.

"Let's go home." I drop my hands and step back. Butcher climbs on his bike, and I climb on behind him. He starts the bike and I snuggle up to him, wrap my arms around his middle, and rest my head on his back.

He takes off and drives out of the parking lot, then onto the highway, but not in the direction of my house.

"Where are we going?" I yell to him so he can hear me over the bike.

"My home."

His house? I'm okay with that. I am curious about where he lives.

eleven

Shaylin

"Holy shit!" I yell as I take in his house. It's huge, for one thing, and it's beautiful. The first part of the house is windows, leaving the living room open. The house is a walnut log home, and I am in love. This is the home I always wanted to have. From the window, I can see the inside of the house is also constructed of walnut logs.

To reach his house we went through a gate and then through a bunch of trees. The house is totally hidden from view, but once we broke through the trees, my breath was taken away.

Butcher shuts off the bike, and I climb off and go back to looking at the house. I can see a six-car garage on one side with a bike, multiple four-wheelers, and his huge truck. Then, farther down, a shed holds a speedboat, houseboat, and jet skis.

I turn back to the house, and I am in awe again. Lights hang from the top of the ceiling. The front of the roof is shaped in a downwards V, and the windows extend all the way up to the roof and surround the front door.

"I love your house, Butcher!" I exclaim.

"Let's go inside." He grabs my hand, and he pulls me along to his house.

We walk up the stairs and he unlocks the door, steps inside, and messes with an iPad on the wall. The inside of the house is just as stunning or more so. It's got this homey, country feel that makes me never want to leave. Everything is solid wood, and the lights have a golden tone to enhance the look of the house. The stair rails are actual logs.

I walk farther into the living room, turn right, and see a dining room, and then I see the kitchen.

I blink a few times, my mouth open wide. This is my dream kitchen. The shelving is solid wood, but the appliances are stainless steel, and in the middle of the kitchen is a huge island made for me to cook on. The kitchen is fully stocked with everything anyone could dream of to bake and cook.

I am in love.

I feel him walk up behind me and I spin around. "I am moving in!"

A grin splits his face and he leans against the wall. "Fine with me."

My mouth pops open in surprise. "I was joking."

He arches an eyebrow before smirking at me. "I wasn't."

Did he just say that? I turn away and leave it at that. I will think about what he just said later. I'm hungry and then I am going to nap, with Butcher. That sounds like heaven. I open the refrigerator door and spot some steaks already thawed out.

"Is it okay if I make us dinner?" I ask Butcher as I rummage through his stuff.

"Have at it, baby."

I stop moving. He called me "baby," and my legs grow weak. This man is going to kill me. I just know it, and he knows it too or he wouldn't say what he does. Cocky bastard.

I plop the steaks down on the island. I search the cabinets, looking through the ingredients he has available. I find some shrimp in the freezer and thaw that out as I make the steaks.

Thirty minutes later I have a meal of steaks topped with parmesan and grilled shrimp with a side of fresh veggies. I walk to the refrigerator, and I grab him a beer and pour myself a glass of wine. I grab a tray and place everything on it. I may or may not want to impress Butcher.

I carry everything to the living room, where Butcher is sitting on the couch staring at the TV. "Food's ready!" He looks up and I smile.

Cooking has always been something that makes me feel better about everything. I don't want to dwell on what happened today, because it was a freak thing.

I place the tray on the coffee table and plop down on the couch next to him. I grab my plate off the tray, scoot back into the couch, and tuck my legs under me.

Under my eyelashes, I watch as Butcher inhales his food, his nostrils flaring as he does so. He cuts into the steak, spears a bite that is smothered in cheese, and places it in his mouth.

He looks over at me. "You're never leaving." He goes back to inhaling his food. My stomach flips over with happiness and giddiness. I always love it when someone likes my food, but it's so much better when it's my man.

We finish our meal, and it's mostly me watching him eat. I love watching people eat, seeing their enjoyment of their food—especially Butcher. Once I am done I place my food on the coffee table, groan, and sit back, holding my too-full stomach. Butcher has been done for a bit now.

"Time for you to sleep." Butcher stands up. Then he bends down, scoops me up, and puts me over his shoulder.

"I don't want to sleep! Put me down, Butcher," I yell at him in mock anger.

Whack! A hand lands on my ass.

"You just smacked me on the ass."

Whack! He hits me harder this time, and I burst out laughing. I pinch his butt cheek and he jumps slightly.

"Shay," he growls, and that's when I feel his hand touching my pussy. He rubs slightly.

"You aren't playing fair!" I yell and he chuckles. He runs up the stairs and I hold onto his shirt, laughing. I love this side of him. I never expected him to be playful.

He bends down and deposits me on the bed. He goes to his closet, and I am not ashamed to admit that I watch his behind as he goes. There is a shirt in his hands when he comes out, and he tosses it to me. "Put this on."

I arch an eyebrow at him. "You're telling me?"

He smirks at me. His wish is my command. As I pull my shirt over my head, I hear his sharp intake of breath, and I lower my head to hide my amusement.

His telling me what to do backfired.

I climb off the bed and turn my back to Butcher. I unbutton my jeans and bend over as I slide them down my butt, making sure to wiggle my hips.

I slide them down my legs and peek over my shoulder at Butcher, who is standing there with a dark expression, his hands clenched at his sides. I grab the shirt off the bed, slide it over my head quickly, and turn to face him. "Thanks for the shirt." I wink and sit back down on the bed.

Butcher

She is perfect but she drives me mad. That fucking striptease she just gave me drove me crazy, and she knows it too. I am in fucking trouble, because she owns me. She has owned me from the first smile.

Now she is sitting on the bed, staring me down with that little smile on her lips, letting me know she knows that she owns me.

Not that I mind.

Now it's time for some fun. Her eyes widen when she takes in my smile and I stalk over to her.

Shaylin

I know that look. He stalks over to me and I know I am in trouble, but the very, very good kind. I lick my lips and press my legs together in anticipation.

"What are you doing, Butcher?" I can't keep my mouth shut and I have to ask.

He ignores me but continues giving me that fucking smile that, in this case, promises a lot of good things, though I have also seen him give men that smile, meaning "you're dead." Butcher is versatile like that, like me.

He gets down onto his knees at the side of the bed and his hands come to my thighs. Oh boy. He grips them between his fingers, and I feel them quiver with need. In a sudden movement, he pulls me to the edge of the bed—to expose me to him—but he sees I have panties on.

"We don't need these." He tsks and his hand wraps around the band at my hip, and then—snap! He tears them from my body again.

"Much better," he growls and looks down at my crotch, taking me in. I flush and lean back on my elbows. He brings his arms up and around my legs then locks his hands together at the top of my pussy, locking me in place. I can't move.

Oh shit! I scream in my mind as I feel the first swipe of his tongue. I intertwine my fingers in his hair and pull at the ends, which causes him to growl, and I shiver. He moves his tongue quicker.

I feel sweat break out at the back of my neck and thighs. This is so intense—there are no words for this. He is unforgiving as he attacks me with vigor, and it's much different than last night. Last night was calculated, him learning what I like. Now he knows where and how to lick.

My body is on edge, my toes curled, reaching the edge of the cliff. His sucks my clit and I moan deeply. That's when I feel his teeth and he bites down slightly.

"AH!" I yell, my body shaking uncontrollably.

I am lifted up and then set down at the top of the bed. I am like a limp noodle. "I believe you are trying to kill me." I laugh and throw my arms above my head, looking at Butcher, who is standing beside me. "Good way to go."

I grab the bottom of his shirt. "Come lie with me." He does as I ask and scoots beside me on the bed. I turn partially on my side and plop my head on his chest. Butcher's hand goes to the back of my head, and he kisses the top of it.

"Sleep, my Shay."

I grin widely when I hear him say I am his Shay. "You're my Butcher." I pull myself closer to his side.

"Damn right." His chest rumbles as he speaks, and I raise my head and kiss his chest directly over his heart. "Sleep, Shay."

I close my eyes and fall into a deep sleep.

Butcher

I arrive at the clubhouse, and I notice everyone else is here already. I don't like Shaylin's house—it's too exposed. Someone can break in as easily as pushing the door in, and I don't like that shit. I don't like her exposed.

I walk to the interrogation room, where I know the fucker is being held. He said some fucked-up shit to Shaylin, and he's going to pay for that.

Nobody fucks with Shaylin.

Everyone in the room turns and looks at me. Smiley takes a few steps in my direction, and I can see his concern for his daughter.

"She's asleep."

"Wore her out, didn't you?"

I freeze and turn around to see who the fuck said that. It was Locke, ever the jokester. I walk over to him and grip him around the throat, squeezing. "Watch your mouth, fucker, if you want to be able to speak out of it again." I push his neck hard, and he hits the wall but does it smiling.

"This is why he can date my kid," Smiley says to everyone and I shake my head. I am not here to fucking chitchat. I am here to fuck him up.

He is hanging in the air by his arms. "I want first hits, Kyle."

Kyle nods. This man is going to get his ass beat by everyone here. He looks me dead in the eye, and I stare back.

I step up in front of him and grip his throat. "Fucked with the wrong woman," I growl and I notice him paling further. I bring my fist back and hit as hard as I can. It flings his head back, and his head rolls forward again.

"She sure was pretty, she looked tight as fuck."

I feel someone come up beside me, and I look over. Smiley is standing beside me with his huge-ass smile.

"You just made this so much more fun," Smiley tells him and I nod.

I take out my knife and run my hand up the edge to gauge the sharpness. I run the tip of the knife along his lips. I don't think I want to hear him speak again. Prying his mouth open with my hand, I motion for Lane to step forward. "Hold his mouth open." Lane grips his mouth, and Smiley has a gun pointed to his head. "Don't move." Smiley smiles at him maniacally.

A pair of pliers is handed to me, and I put it in his mouth. I grip his tongue and pull it. Gripping my knife, I press it against his tongue and he starts pulling away.

"Should have watched your mouth." I pull hard and the piece of tongue hits the floor.

"Who's next?" I step back, and Lane steps forward and beats the shit out of him. One by one everyone gets a piece of him, especially the members of Lane's club. She is their princess.

"Have fun in hell," Smiley tells him and brings his gun up and pulls the trigger. The fucker slumps over, dead.

"I'm out." I turn on my heel and walk back the way I came. Shay is at my home waiting on me.

The Next Day

Shaylin

I know my bakery is clean and will be like nothing happened, but I dread seeing the place where everything went down.

Butcher pulls to a stop outside the bakery, and he climbs off first then I follow him. He tucks me into his side, and we walk together to the front door.

Today I am interviewing some ladies who will come work with me full time. I take my keys out of my pocket and unlock my door. I step inside and then I'm immediately pulled back. I eye Butcher in confusion.

He takes his hand off my forearm. "Let me check the place out."

I nod and cross my arms across my chest, and he searches the bakery, including the kitchen and bathroom. Once he is finished, he nods in my direction, letting me know everything is okay.

I walk back to the kitchen and grab the containers of measured-out ingredients that I have pre-planned. For the next two hours, I get everything ready for the day and set up the glass showcase with the extras in the back.

"Butcher, will you turn the sign to open for me, sweetheart?" I don't look up from organizing everything. When I don't hear him moving, I look up to see what he is doing and, much to my surprise, he is standing at the door, looking directly at me.

"What is it?" I ask and stand back up.

"Nothing." He unlocks the door, and I catch a small smile.

He liked me calling him sweetheart.

I grab the last cupcake off the tray and place it inside the showcase, and then I put down the glass door.

"Butcher..." I start and his hands wrap around my hips, pulling me back. My back hits his hard front, and I am pulled into his lap. I laugh, lean back, and press my lips to his.

His hand twines through my hair, and he presses me harder against him to deepen the kiss. A loud rumble comes from him, and I shiver at the sound. I love that I affect him.

I realize, in this moment, I want to cross that next step with him. I want to give him that part of me. I turn in his lap so I can reach him better. A hand grips my ass and I jump in shock, which causes me to rub against his dick.

He pulls his lips from mine and kisses the side of my neck. "Fuck me," he whispers and I know he is trying to control himself.

So I take the plunge. "I will tonight." I twist my hands together in my lap in anticipation as I eye his reaction.

His mouth opens slightly. He takes deep breaths and cups the side of my face. "Shay, you don't have to."

I soften my gaze and touch the hand resting on my cheek. "I want you," I whisper and touch my forehead to his. "Only you."

"My Shay." His voice is rough and I lean forward, pressing my lips to his cheek, right on the scar.

"My Butcher."

The bell above the door dings, bringing us out of the moment, and I rise from his lap. Butcher keeps his hand on my back, and the only emotions I feel right now are peace and happiness. It feels like I have been missing something my whole life, and now it feels like I found the missing link and that link is Butcher.

He came into my life in an unusual circumstance and was not what I had expected at all. I was eating lunch and he came into the steak house, saw me, and never left.

I never wanted him to leave.

There was something about him that was haunted and he was frightening, but I was never scared of him. But I know a lot of people are afraid of him—I can see their reactions.

"Hi!" As I greet the customer, I realize it's the guy whose head I busted the tip jar over when he grabbed my arm.

Fuck me, man. Can this get any worse? I don't think.

"Henry, what are you doing here?" They aren't beating around the bush with me today. I am not in the mood, and I also don't understand why he is here. I broke a tip jar over his head.

"I came here to see about that date." Henry presses himself hard against the counter, leaning toward me.

"Henry, I have a man." Butcher tightens his grip on me, and I know I made him happy saying that.

Henry glares at me. Does he not see the man standing behind me? I am in his arms. If Henry doesn't put that together, there is something wrong with him.

"I don't care. It's one date," he begs, and I cringe when I get a whiff of his breath. I don't even want to comprehend what is going on there. That is not everyday morning breath. It smells like shit and god knows what.

Butcher growls loudly and lets go of me. Oh man.

"Henry, leave—before you get your ass beat."

Henry falls onto the counter, holding his hands together. "Please, my...my...Shay."

Butcher is around the counter and has Henry by the throat before I can blink. "She's *my* Shaylin. Never speak her name again."

Well, that was hot.

"I'm sorry. I will leave," Henry says, defeated, and Butcher lets him go. Henry walks to his Mercedes, which still shocks me. He can afford a Mercedes, but not soap?

Butcher goes into the bathroom to wash his hands and scrub his body.

A woman walks into the bakery and straight up to the counter. "I am here for the interview."

"Hi! I'm Shaylin. Come with me. We can sit down and talk through everything." Butcher comes out of the bathroom. "Would you mind watching the store while I..." The girl is freaking out, and my eyes widen as she runs back out of the store.

What the fuck?

I feel like tracking her ass down and beating some sense into her. That's insulting and disrespectful.

"I like it when you get mad."

His words bring me from my thoughts. I arch an eyebrow and cock my hip to the side. "You do, huh?"

He winks at me and my heart skips a beat. I swoon at the sight of that wink. He tortures me with it, and he knows what to do to get me going.

twelve

Later That Night

Tonight is the night, and the nerves are getting to me, to be honest. I am at Butcher's house right now, and he is at the gate picking up the pizza we ordered.

I am terrified that I will be bad in bed and that it won't be good for him. Hello, Virgin Mary here. I know it's going to hurt, but that's not the biggest thing.

Sex is such an intimate thing, and I have waited a long time for this to happen—and it's all going down in a couple of hours.

I hear the door open and look around, and Butcher walks inside. My belly growls as the scent hits me. I am starving. He sets the pizza down on the coffee table, and I flip back the top and grab a slice. He sits down beside me and dives in.

We sit in silence and I want to say something, but what do I say? I feel like I should be cool and just let it happen. Then the other side of me wants to say something, but I don't know what. I'm just a mess.

Smallville comes on and I grab the remote to turn it up.

"Pussy," he says to me.

My mouth pops open, and I glare at Butcher in mock anger. "What did you say about my show?"

"Pussy," he mocks and I snort. It's hilarious when he tries to be funny.

He bursts out laughing and I drop my pizza. I have never heard him laugh like that before. I watch in awe as he laughs loudly and deeply. This is amazing.

Once he is done laughing, I press a kiss to his lips quickly and then go back to my pizza. I am so infatuated with him.

For the next thirty minutes we finish eating, and he gets up to throw away the pizza. I look at the clock on the wall, and it says eight o'clock.

I am ready.

I stand up and take my shirt off, and I throw it toward the kitchen. Then I walk to the stairs. I take off my bra and place it on the stair rail.

I hurry up the stairs and, at the top, I take off my jeans. I lay them down, and when I reach the entrance to his bedroom, I take off my panties and drape them over the door handle.

Oh my god. I can't believe I've just done that. I know he has seen me naked before, but this is just different.

Hands touch my hips and I jump. I spin around and come face to face with Butcher. His hands move up my sides and then under my arms. He lifts me off the ground, and my legs go around his waist.

His face is intense as he takes in my naked body. I raise my face, press my lips to his, and run my hands down his back.

I feel the bed pressed against my back, and my stomach flips. He presses his lips harder against mine, his tongue twining with mine. His hands run up and down my sides, goose bumps breaking out across my naked flesh.

Then his fingers move from my hip to the edge of my pussy, and I gasp in his mouth. He is teasing me. He chuckles, and I move my hips over in hopes that his hand will move closer to where I need it to be.

He does what I need, and his finger strokes my clit. I moan into his mouth, and he moves his finger again in a slow circle.

The finger moves from my clit to my opening, and I relax as he slides a finger inside. "Soaked," he growls in my mouth, and I raise my hips, his finger slipping farther inside. He presses his finger all the way in and slowly brings it back out. I curl my toes and throw my head back.

He kisses along my throat, and I feel him add another finger. He slowly presses them inside of me, and I wince slightly because his fingers are way bigger than mine. His thumb presses against my clit.

I hiss in pleasure and raise my hips, letting him press farther inside of me. His lips move from my throat to my breasts. He licks the tip of my nipple then sucks it deep into his mouth.

His fingers quicken inside of me, and I feel myself getting closer. His thumb presses harder against my clit, and I am right on the edge. I gasp and dig my nails into his back, and I raise my left leg up his hip, giving him better access.

His lips wrap around my nipple again, and his fingers curl inside of me, hitting the spot.

"Butcher!" I hiss and wrap my arms around him tightly, my body shaking.

He slides out of bed. His large hands grip the bottom of his shirt, and he pulls it over his head, and I drink in the sight of him shirtless. He has such a great body. His pants join his shirt and then his underwear.

Then it hits me.

This is really happening.

He reaches into the night stand and pulls out a condom. This is really happening. He climbs into bed with me, and my hands start to shake. I sit up and take the condom from his hand. I open the package and put the condom on him.

I lie back on the bed and stare into Butcher's eyes. His face is softer and more relaxed than I have ever seen him.

He crawls up between my legs, and his elbows go to either side of my head. I reach up and touch his jaw. "I'm ready."

He nods and kisses me on the forehead. I feel his dick touching my entrance, and I relax my body totally.

Butcher reaches down and grabs my hand, then grabs the other. He raises them above my head, and I suck in a deep breath. He doesn't move his forehead from mine, and we stare deep into each other's eyes.

"I don't want to hurt you," he confesses and I melt.

"I don't care about that, I just want you. I want all of you."

He closes his eyes at my words, and I feel him pressing. I close my eyes tightly, taking in deep breaths.

He slides in an inch and it starts to get uncomfortable. "Just do it."

"Shay," he starts to argue.

My hand is on the back of his neck. "I'm okay, just do it."

He does what I ask. He slides all the way in with one smooth, solid movement. "Fuck." I turn my head to the side as tears form in my eyes.

"I can't take this shit," Butcher growls, and I open my eyes in time to see him slam his fist into the headboard.

"I'm okay, it's better now," I reassure him and take the hand that hit the head board. "I promise." It is, I just feel very full and there is a bite of pain, but it's not bad. He brings his hand down and touches my clit. He rubs in slow circles, and the pain is immediately gone.

"Much better." My voice deepens with pleasure.

"I can't believe." He stops talking and stares down at me in awe.

"You can't believe?"

"That you're mine." He kisses me, and it's such a tender, loving kiss that tears form in my eyes again, this time from pure happiness.

"Butcher," I say with such raw emotion, and he starts moving. I moan when he hits the spot inside of me that drives me crazy.

That spurs him to go faster, and I raise my hands above my head and press them against the headboard. He growls and licks my throat. "Come for me." He twists his hips and hits the spot again.

"Oh shit," I gasp. I thought him going down on me was intense, but this is a whole different thing.

His teeth nip my lips and my throat, and I feel his finger on my clit again. Then a sharp pinch and I come.

"Oh god, Butcher." I grip whatever the hell I can as my body quivers uncontrollably, and I feel him coming along with me. My leg slides from his hip onto the bed. "Let's do that again tomorrow."

I feel him shake with laughter and I grin. I got what I wanted.

He slides out of me, and I cringe at the slight pain. Butcher isn't a small guy, and pain was going to happen—there wasn't any way around it.

He takes the condom, ties it off, and throws it in the trashcan beside the bed. He rolls over onto his back and takes me with him—I'm lying on top of him. My head is on his chest, my legs on either side of his body.

We lie in silence, my eyes starting to droop closed, because he is running his hand up and down my back, which relaxes me.

"I lost my parents and my brother when I was eighteen. My twin brother. I lost all of them at once in a car accident, and I came upon the scene a few minutes later, because I wanted to follow them in my new truck."

My heart is hurting right now. I lie completely still, letting him tell me what he needs to.

"I will never forget seeing the people I loved most in the world dead, their eyes blank. They were just gone, when they were alive just minutes earlier."

"I had the funeral and then I joined the navy. I rarely spoke unless I had to. I was just dead inside, and I continued to be that way until you, my Shay. You made me feel for the first time in a long time. It fucking eats at me when you leave my sight, because I can't stand the thought of something happening to you."

Don't cry, Shaylin. Tears pool in my eyes, and I suck my lips into my mouth. I have never felt pain like this. I have never hurt for someone before like I have for Butcher.

"A mission went wrong after I became a SEAL, and I was tortured for two days before I was rescued. I got demons, Shay, but you make that shit less haunting. Your light keeps them at bay."

I'm done.

I sob against his chest, and I hold him as tight as I can. "Butcher, I am so sorry." I raise my head and press my lips against his, holding his jaw in my hand. I kiss him with such emotion, letting how I feel about him come through. "I will never leave you, Butcher," I tell him through kisses. I take my lips from his and kiss the scar on his cheek. "I will take all of your demons, Butcher, as long as I get to have you."

He gives me a look that I can't decipher, and I spot the next scar and kiss it. "Your scars are hauntingly beautiful, they make you who you are."

He flips me onto my back and presses his face into the crook of my neck. I wrap my arms around his neck and just hold him.

I will never let go.

thirteen

"What are we doing here?" I ask Butcher as we pull up outside a gun shop and shooting range.

He turns to look at me. "Spoiling you."

"Butcher!" I smack him lightly on the shoulder. I told him that I love guns, I always carry one on me, and I've got some stashed everywhere. I think back to the robbery, and I'm glad I had one stuffed under the shelf.

He steps out of his truck, slams the door shut, and walks over to the passenger side to open the door. I lean toward him, wrap my arms around his neck, and squeeze him. He steps back and I don't let go—I wrap my legs around his waist. He chuckles and digs his fingers into my sides and I squirm, laughing. His lips press into mine—halting my laughter—and I open my mouth, deepening the kiss.

Someone honks their horn and I pull away slightly, kiss the side of his mouth, and hop down. Butcher puts his hand on the small of my back and, as always, he looks around the area to make sure there aren't any threats.

He opens the door to the gun shop and I step in, and Butcher follows me. I look around the room, and the man behind the counter smiles at us. "Ah, Butcher, we have the gun you ordered." He grabs a case that is tiffany blue, like the gun I wanted.

No way. Butcher is already staring at me. The man behind the counter opens the case. My mouth pops open. It's the gun I wanted! The tiffany blue gun that I have been looking at for the past couple of months.

"I love it!" I turn around and squeeze his middle tightly, shaking him from side to side slightly. "I can't believe you bought me a gun. Thank you."

He just chuckles, and I let him go and turn around to look at the pistol that is waiting on me.

The man behind the counter smiles at both of us. "Let me show you how..." he says, but I already have the gun out of the case.

"I got it." I smile.

I check the chamber and grab a loaded magazine. I slide it in, slide back the chamber, and put the safety on. "Let's go shoot." I grin and grab the tiffany blue holster that came with it. I put the gun it in and snap the holster on my side.

"I...I...all right," he stammers, and I feel Butcher pressing up against my back.

His breath hits my ear. "Fuck me, Shay, you're going to kill me."

I laugh under my breath and turn my head from side to side, smirking at him.

"Behave." Butcher's hand taps my ass lightly.

"What is that?" I mock and step away from him, which causes him to growl.

"Follow me." The worker motions for us, and I see Butcher grabbing the rest of my stuff for me.

Butcher

Why the fuck must men look at her? The fucking man who owns the damn store hasn't been able to take his eyes off of her since she showed him she knows how to work a gun. It makes me ready to kill every fucker around.

"Here you are." He motions to a booth, and she steps past him, going straight up to it, and puts on earmuffs.

I set the rest of her stuff on the floor beside her and stand back up, eyeing the man who won't take his eyes off of her. He's pretending to watch her form, which is perfect. He reaches out to touch her hips, pretending to correct her, which pisses me the fuck off. I bring my own gun out and point it at him. "Don't you fucking dare."

He snaps to attention and backs away from her, and he throws his hands up in the air. "I wasn't meaning anything."

I roll my eyes and look at him like he is the dumbest shit in the world. "You haven't taken your eyes off of her since we got here. I would advise you to leave." The gun is still pointed at him. I motion toward the door, and he goes away.

Pussy.

I slide my gun back in my holster and lean against the wall, watching as she prepares and double checks her gun. She's too fucking sexy for her own good.

She catches me looking and shoots me a blinding smile. I can't fucking believe she is mine. I must have fucking done some kind of good in my life.

She takes the ear muffs off and turns to look at me. "You know there is a mirror there, right?" I follow her eyes and I know she caught me.

She laughs and puts the ear muffs back on and braces herself to shoot. She raises her gun and fires six shots almost simultaneously. She hits the button on the wall to bring her target up to us, and I step closer to take a look. Three shots to the head and three to the heart.

Fucking lethal.

Shaylin

I caught Butcher and it was hilarious. He tried to be slick and hide what he was doing from me. He was telling the worker off for checking me out—Butcher style, which consists of a gun pointed to the head.

Isn't he just perfect? I sound crazy, but when did I ever claim to be normal?

"I'm hungry," I tell Butcher as we walk out to his truck.

"Where do you want to eat?" He opens the door for me. I reach up to grab the oh-shit handle, and he pushes my butt to give me a boost.

"Blues?"

He nods and shuts the door behind me.

Later That Night

Shaylin

"Shay?" Butcher calls from outside the bathroom door. I am getting ready for a large bonfire cookout thing at the Devil Souls MC clubhouse. To say that I am nervous is an understatement. I know all of the girls, but it's way different now because of us being officially together.

"Yeah?" I open the bathroom door and stick my head out.

I gasp in shock at what I see. He is standing there with a vest with my name on it that says "Property Of Butcher." If you don't know the significance of this, in the biker world, it's the same thing as marriage.

This is a big deal.

"Butcher," I choke out as tears flood my eyes.

Butcher steps forward, looking angry. "Don't cry, Shay, it kills me when you cry."

Oh my god. He is literally trying to kill me. I widen the distance between us and press my lips to his, my tears falling onto both of our cheeks. I am falling in love with this man. He doesn't say much, but when he does? It rocks my world

There is so much more to Butcher than what everyone sees. What I see is my Butcher. My Butcher is badass and dangerous, scary to the core, but I see a different part of him.

I pull back from him and grab the vest from his hand. He brings his large, scarred-up hand up to my cheekbone and wipes away my tears. The same hands that can kill someone in a few seconds, but to me his touch is gentle.

How lucky am I? I am so lucky to have him. He may think it's the other way around—and he has told me so—but I am the lucky one. Everything about him is perfect to me.

I slide my arms into the vest. I smile at him widely. I love the feel of it on me. I pull my hair out and let it drape over one shoulder, and I slowly turn around, letting him take a look. Facing him, I smirk. "How does it look?"

He grabs my hips and pulls me to him, and our hips collide. "My name looks good on you." The hand on my hip glides down to my ass and squeezes.

I throw my head back, laughing. "We better get going or we are going to be late." I check the clock for emphasis and step out of his arms to slip on my boots.

"I will be outside."

"Okay, baby."

He stops, and I bite my lip to hold back my laughter. "Your ass is mine when we get home."

He walks out of the room, and I laugh under my breath. I love messing with him.

I am sore after last night, but I am not going to let that stop me. I want him too much. Last night was one of the best nights of my life, and it was sure one of the happiest. I have never felt so content before, and that's all because of one silent and broody man who stalked me. How does that sound for a fairy tale?

I take one last look at myself in the mirror, taking a extra second to admire my vest. Smiling at my reflection I bend down and slip on my boots before walking down the stairs and outside to my man.

Butcher

Fuck. I didn't know outsiders were invited to the party tonight— and this usually doesn't happen—but to make it seem like we aren't total criminals, we let people come inside for a bit then kick them out.

I park my bike and climb off. Shaylin is looking toward the field where the party is being held. I take this moment to admire her, and it's looking like I should take her home. She could wear a sack over her head, and they would find something else to admire.

"Butcher! Over here." Vin is standing at the edge of the field waving me over.

I thank god her property patch came in, or I wouldn't let her in. There are some pretty pussy boys who come to these parties to seem like billy bad asses.

Shaylin puts her small hand on my shoulder, bringing me from my thoughts. She climbs off the bike and tucks herself into my side. "Let's go see your friends."

Growling under my breath, I do as she asks.

We walk across the field, and I see fuckers staring at her then at her patch and down at the ground. That's right, fuckers, eyes on the ground if you want to keep them.

"Bitches." I tear my gaze from the pussy boys and follow Shay's gaze to some want-to-be ole ladies in the corner of the field. I feel Shaylin's hand slide from my hip to my back pocket, and she grabs my ass.

I just got claimed.

Shaylin

I just claimed Butcher, and he knows it too, because a large smile spread across his face. Those hookers in the corner were looking him up and down.

I didn't like that.

These skanks are women who want MC men. The men don't touch them, because these women want to use them and the MC men don't like that. So the skanks show up at these open parties, and then they leave because no one pays them any mind, which pisses them off. These men don't like easy.

"Hey, Shaylin!" Jean yells across the field, and I tear my eyes from the skanks.

"Hi Jean!" I say once we get close to her.

She eyes me up and down and looks at Butcher before giving me a blinding smile. "We need to talk!" she practically yells and grabs my hand, attempting to pull me from Butcher, who holds fast and growls deeply.

Jean rolls her eyes at him. "We are just sitting on the couch by the fire." She motions to the other girls and he lets go, but I can tell he doesn't want to.

"I will be okay. I got Tiff." I wink and pat my back. His face softens, and I can see the amused glint in his eyes.

"Tiff?" Jean asks as we step away from Butcher, and I grin at her. "My gun."

We walk together to the group of ole ladies sitting on the couch, and a club member stands on either side of the couch. My uncles' women are never left unprotected, because we have enemies. We live beside the ocean and people want to use our town to funnel in drugs. This brings us up against some scary people. But I refuse to have a bodyguard. My father agreed because I live outside of the county and I'm in Devil Souls jurisdiction.

My dad is a sucker and I gave him the pouty eyes. I wish my dad would find himself someone to spend the rest of his life with. I know he loved my mom, but I don't think it was the all-consuming kind, not someone who he was meant to grow old with. My dad deserves that. He spent his whole life raising us kids and only worried about us. We were his life, and now it's time for him to live his life for himself. He should have been doing this for years, but I think he just needs a push. Maybe I will set him up on a blind date, but do I want to be murdered?

"Hi Shaylin!" four different voices ring out, and I wave at them. Jean pulls me down beside Alisha, who is getting prettier by the second. It should be a crime how pretty she is. Hell, every one of these women could easily pass for a model.

"I see you are now an ole lady." Chrystal nods at my vest.

I grin ear to ear as I think back to when he gave it to me earlier. "Yeah, I am."

Alisha pulls me into a hug, and then another girl takes her place hugging me and welcoming me to the family. These women are genuine. You don't get that with a lot of people.

"I have been meaning to call, but I need to order a cake and cupcakes for my daughter's birthday party coming up in a month."

"Text me the details and I will book you in," I tell her.

I look around and see Butcher talking to Techy, but he is staring directly at me. I blow him a kiss, and he ducks his head to hide his smile.

"I never thought I would see the day when Butcher would be brought to his knees," Jean says and I shrug.

"He brought me to mine too," I tell her and they all say, "Aww."

"So you fucked him yet?"

I laugh at how blunt she is. "Yeah." My mind wanders and I visualize him above me, moving inside of me. Stop, Shaylin, save it for later.

"How big is it?" Jean whispers and her eyes widen. All the other girls scoot closer.

"I didn't really measure." I move toward them. "It hurt like a bitch—and he is as wide as my wrist, at least."

Alisha looks at me in sympathy. "Techy is ten inches, so I get it."

I wince and scoot back on the couch so I am facing the party, and my eyes gravitate to Butcher. I see a skank standing right behind him.

Oh, hell no. She better stay right where she's at.

"Did you ever find someone to come work for you?"

I tear my gaze from Butcher to look at the girls. I shake my head. "No, sadly."

Kayla perks up. "Paisley, Torch's daughter, is looking for a summer job."

"Tell her to come in whenever she can and we can talk it over."

"Thank you!"

I look back at Butcher, and what I see makes my blood burn like fire. She is touching his arm, and he pulls away sharply and backs away from her. She moves closer to him, and she is going to touch him again.

That isn't going to fly with me.

I stand up and stomp over to them. Jean yells, "Oh shit!" and the other girls cheer. The bitch knew I came here with him.

Butcher

She is pissed. She glares at the girl who was hitting on me, walks past her, and wraps herself around me.

I fucking love this shit.

Shaylin smiles smugly at the girl, and it takes everything in me not to laugh. The girl glares at Shaylin, before opening her mouth. "What's your deal?" Her snotty, babyish voice irks my nerves right off the bat.

"You were hitting on my man. What the fuck is your deal?" Shaylin steps closer to the girl.

"Like I give a fuck?" She looks me up and down, and I blink in disbelief. "I can have him on top of me." She snaps her fingers. My thoughts go back to the fucker who said something similar about Shaylin.

I step out from behind Shaylin, ready to tell the girl off. Why would I touch something like that when I got my Shay? Does she not see what I have? Women.

Shaylin smiles a huge-ass smile.

Fuck.

"You shouldn't have said that." Shaylin grins at her.

The girl looks confused. "What are you going to d—" She doesn't finish the word before Shaylin is on her ass, punching her in the mouth.

"Ugly bitch! All of these women here are ugly!"

Shaylin bursts out laughing, and the girl stands up to face her.

"I really didn't feel like fighting today. I just wanted to have fun with my man and the ole ladies. Now you have fucking disrespected them and hit on my man. You're asking to get your ass beat. No hair pulling, I can't stand that." Shaylin points at her in warning and goes back to grinning.

The girl brings her hand toward Shaylin's hair. Shay catches her hand and bends it backwards, and the girl screams. "I told you no hair!" Shay brings her free hand to the girl's throat and pushes her down, and the girl lands on her back.

"Who is under who now?" Shaylin cackles.

"Man, your woman is crazy," Vinny says and I look at him, grinning.

"I know."

Vinny bursts out laughing. "Both of y'all are crazy."

I am not denying shit.

"Apologize to the ladies."

"Fuck you, bitch."

Shaylin sighs dramatically and flips her hair over her shoulder. "Damn, I was hoping for the easy way out." She smacks her hard across the face. "You need to learn some manners. Apologize." Shay turns the woman's head so she's facing the girls, who are watching, amused.

"No."

"You're really pissing me off." She slides her hand up from the girl's neck and cups her face. Then she slams her head on the ground. "Do it now."

"I'm sorry!"

"Good girl." Shaylin is still grinning like a loon. She pats the woman's face hard. "Now all you gotta do is tell my man you will never look at him again because if you do I will cut out your eyes."

"You're crazy!" the girl screams. Shaylin rolls her eyes, and her hand goes back to the girl's throat. "Tell me something I don't know. Now go on." She waves her hand in my direction and winks at me.

She is perfect.

"I will never look at you again or your girlfriend will cut my eyes out."

I shake with laughter, and I hear people around us doing the same.

Shaylin stands up and takes the girl with her. "I'm taking out the trash. I will be back." She half drags the girl by the throat to the gate and lets her go. Then she kicks her on the ass, and the girl falls a few feet away.

"Butcher, I think she is crazier than you," Jean says.

"She is perfect, isn't she?"

Shaylin walks straight to me, and I watch her body move with every step. I am only so fucking strong. I walk to her and throw her over my shoulder. I need my woman.

Shaylin

I am thrown over his shoulder and I smack his ass, which causes him to retaliate. His hand lands on my ass hard.

People catcall all around us, and Butcher moves into the woods behind the clubhouse. He walks for a bit until we are out of sight of everyone. Butcher slides me down his body, and my feet hit the ground.

I am backed up against a tree with him towering over me. "You're too fucking hot, Shay." He slams his mouth onto mine as I gasp. His hand fists my hair, pulling slightly. I moan in delight at him being aggressive.

I feel his hands at the button of my pants. This is so thrilling. I am about to have sex with a hundred people just across the field. I feel my zipper being lowered, and I push his hands away. I drag my pants, along with my panties, down my legs leaving me open and bare for the world. I bite his lip and pull his hair, pulling my upper half closer to him. A hand snakes between my legs, and I almost fall to the ground.

"Soaked," he growls and presses me hard against the tree. I unbuckle his belt, unbutton his pants, and push them down, along with his underwear, freeing him.

His tongue moves against mine, and I clamp my teeth down on it and grab his dick. He hisses and tears my hand away. He lifts me off the ground, and I wrap my legs around his waist.

He bends down slightly, and I feel his dick at my entrance. I shudder with pleasure at the feel. I open my eyes and break my lips from his, and I lay the back of my head against the tree. His teeth skim my neck as he presses inside of me, which causes a slight pinch of pain.

I dig my heels in and raise my hips so he has better access. My back arches as he slides farther inside of me and, once he is fully inside, I gasp and arch my toes. I have never felt anything so good. There is nothing better than to be filled fully.

"So fucking sexy." He brings his hips back and slams back inside me.

"Fuck." I gasp and drag my nails down his bare back. He hisses in pain and then slams inside again, harder this time. I love it.

"Faster." I moan and kiss the side of his neck. He does what I ask.

Minutes, hours, seconds—I am not aware of time. All I know is Butcher and the feel of him moving inside of me. It's something I know I will never tire of. This isn't just fucking. Every touch, every movement means something.

Butcher means something to me, and I know I am falling in love with him. I think I have been for a while, but now it truly hits me. Tears fill my eyes, and I close them before he sees. I bring my lips to his and kiss him with every emotion I am feeling but not saying.

He strokes my clit, and I cry out loudly as I come hard, clamping down on his dick. I feel him come a second later, filling me.

Wait.

He didn't wear a condom. I open my eyes wide and look at Butcher, who has completely stilled. "I am on birth control."

"I am clean, there hasn't been a woman besides you in many years, and I just got tested a month ago."

He kisses my sweaty forehead and I move away from the tree, wrapping my arms around his neck.

"Ready to go home?"

I nod and he sets me down on the ground. I bend down and grab my panties, cleaning myself as much as possible before slipping on my jeans. I watch Butcher's white ass disappear into his jeans.

He grabs my hand, and we walk through the woods to his bike. I am not wanting to face the crowd right now with my sex hair and cum running down my leg. Not attractive.

We come out of the woods and head for his bike, and I see the skank is still hanging around outside of the gate. Butcher hands me the helmet and I slip it on. I move my hair to one side and button the snap.

Butcher climbs on and I follow him. His hands wrap around my knees, and he pulls me flush against his back. I laugh and wrap my arms around his middle, and my lips find the side of his neck.

He starts the bike and, as we pull out toward the gate, we pass the girl who I beat up earlier. I give her the one-finger salute. I feel Butcher shaking with laughter. The girl obviously has no common sense.

We arrive back at his house about fifteen minutes later. His house is even more beautiful at night because of the golden light coming from inside, enhancing the interior.

"We should go boating tomorrow." I look over to the shed that has the jet skis and the speedboat.

"Fine with me." He climbs off.

"I think you're trying to spoil me?" I flash him a sheepish smile. He bought me the gun that I had been eyeing for months, and I just found out the whole collection will be in soon, including a higher powered rifle.

He arches an eyebrow. "Is it working?" He picks up my hand and helps me off the bike.

"Oh yeah."

He kisses my temple. "Then I am doing something right."

I am swooning right now—he is so sweet! He twines our fingers together, and we walk up the steps to the house. He unlocks the door and we walk inside.

"Grab something to eat and I will run you a bath."

I grab the waistband of his pants, pulling him toward me.

"Only if you join me."

He kisses my forehead, but I catch a small smile. His hand lands on my ass and I jump. "Behave."

I roll my eyes at him. "Honey, do you think that is possible? When am I ever good?" A finger runs down the middle of his chest.

"Shay," he growls in warning, but it doesn't faze me. I will let him think he won because I do want that hot bath because I am sore, not that I will tell him that. He punched a hole in the headboard last night—it was a total breaking down moment.

The stairs creak as Butcher walks up the steps, and I shuffle over the refrigerator to find cold pizza. Nothing better than cold pizza. I grab my bottle of wine also. Aren't I winning in life?

After I finish my pizza, I walk upstairs with my bottle of wine and a glass. I've got to make myself look semi-normal and not drink out of the bottle like I want to.

I cut across his bedroom to the bathroom, which is huge—and the massive tub is to die for. The bathroom is bathed in a soft glow that gives it a very romantic feel.

Butcher has his back to me, stark naked. I take a moment to admire the view of his backside and the tattoos covering his back. He looks over his shoulder at me and walks over to the tub, steps in, and slides into the water. I never thought a man could look so sexy in a tub, but my man isn't normal.

I slip my cut off and lay it gently on the counter. Then I bring my shirt over my head, unsnap my bra, and toss them both on the floor. Then I unbutton my jeans and slide them down my legs, leaving me naked.

"Damn," Butcher mutters under his breath, and I wink at him.

I step into the steaming bathtub.

"Your back to me." I look at him in confusion, but I turn around so my back is to him. I sink down into the water and close my eyes. This feels amazing. His hand drifts down my back, and he pours water down my back, wetting the bottom half of my hair.

"What are you doing?"

"Let me care for you," he whispers, and his hand smooths my wet hair down my back. "Lean your head back."

I lean my head back, and he pours a cup of water over my head but doesn't get any on my face. He does this a couple more times before I hear a bottle opening, and I crane my neck to see he has a shampoo bottle in hand.

The smell of my vanilla shampoo hits my nose. I hold completely still. His hand touches the middle of my head, digging his fingers in to massage it. I lean my head back, giving him better access.

This is heaven. I sigh and brace my hand against his knee. For the next fifteen minutes, Butcher washes my hair, conditions it, and washes my body.

I have never felt so cherished in my entire life.

After he carries me to bed, both of us still naked, he gently lays me down on the bed and climbs in beside me. I sit up and push on his shoulder, making him lie down flat on his back, and I bring my leg over his hip, straddling him.

"You made me feel more special earlier than I have ever felt in my whole entire life." I drag my hands from his stomach to his chest, and my finger strokes the scar above the middle of his chest.

"You are special, Shay."

I close my eyes; my nose burns with tears. "You say you aren't sweet, sweetheart."

"Just to you." He chuckles and his hands slide along my legs, stopping once he gets to my inner thighs.

Opening my eyes I bend down and kiss the long jagged scar. Then I move to the next, the next, and the next. I kiss what people would call imperfections, but they are what make Butcher who he is.

"You are perfect." I kiss the scar on his cheekbone, and I feel him shake his head. I lay my forehead against his, looking into his eyes. "You're perfect for me. We are both crazy." I laugh and he laughs along with me. I will never grow tired of him smiling and laughing.

I have noticed that the shadow in his eyes isn't there. When I look into his eyes, I see happiness. I put that there. I make it my mission to make him happy. He deserves that and so much more.

I could ramble about this forever because I just really care about him. I care about him, and I am not afraid to show that. Call me cheesy but I am not hiding who I am.

fourteen

Shaylin

My father managed to bribe me into going to dinner at his house with Butcher since I told him that we are officially a couple now and I got a cut.

I probably should be nervous but, on the other hand, I want my father to see Butcher the way I do. Don't get me wrong—Butcher is a scary and dangerous man. I see the way he gets murderous every time a man checks me out. I literally grab onto his hand so he doesn't deck him.

That is just who he is—he is a very possessive and protective person. I get why he is like that because it affected him when he lost his family, and the thought of something happening to me panics him.

We pull up outside Dad's house, and I see Lane is already here, in his truck since he has my niece with him. I can't wait to see her! It's been a month, and I have never gone that long.

After climbing off, I stand beside the bike waiting on Butcher to get off.

"Smiles."

I hear Butcher chuckling, and I look over to see Dad staring at both of us in amusement. Rolling my eyes I walk through the yard to my daddy, who has stepped off the porch. I sink into his arms and he hugs me tightly to him. It never gets old being hugged by your father.

"He been treating you well or do I got to kill a fucker today?" he says very loudly, and I know Butcher heard him.

I smack his back and step out of his arms, giving him the stink eye. "You think I would need you to kill someone if they did me wrong?"

My dad smiles widely. "That's my Smiles."

Crazy, I tell you.

He turns around and walks back up the steps. "Food is on the table, I got shit catered in."

We follow him and Butcher settles in beside me, his hand on the small of my back before it falls away and he smacks my ass. I yelp and grab his hand so he can't do that again.

"Do that shit again and I will kill you." My dad doesn't turn around but continues walking into the house.

I stand up on my tiptoes and Butcher bends down. "Do it again and no pussy for you."

Butcher pulls back and gives me a look that says I am full of shit. I may be, but he can pretend to grovel for a bit.

We step inside the house and I hear a shrill scream. Tiffany runs into the room and Lane follows her. I bend down and she slams into me. I teeter backwards but Butcher puts his hand on my back, catching me.

She lets me go and smiles up at Butcher.

"Hi, kid."

She squints at his hand and makes a tsking sound. "You need some clear coat. I just got done with Grandpa's."

I burst out laughing. These men can face anything, but they can't deal with the wrath of this little girl. She takes his hand and leads him over to the large leather couch. He looks back at me with widened eyes that say "help."

I just wave bye to him, and he gives me a look that says I am getting it later. I walk over to Lane, who is standing just inside the doorway to the kitchen watching his daughter and Butcher. "Shay, come here."

I walk past Lane into the kitchen, where my dad is setting the food out on the table. "Yeah, Dad?"

He gives me a hard and serious look. I know there is some stuff going on right now. "What's the matter, Dad?" I step closer to him.

"The cartel is trying to funnel drugs through our town, but this a different group, they are dangerous. Carry a gun at all times."

I let out a deep breath and nod. My gun is on the small of my back. I grab it from the holster and show it to him. He grins when he sees the tiffany blue gun. "When did you get that?"

"Butcher got it for me a couple days ago."

My dad looks puzzled for a second before he starts laughing. "What is it?" I wrinkle my nose and put my gun back.

"What pawn shop was it?"

"It was slightly out of town. Why?"

He laughs again. I look over my shoulder at Lane, wondering if he knows what's going on, and he is laughing too.

"You going to tell me what is going on?" I cross my arms across my chest.

"We own that pawn shop, darling. We got a call from the manager, and he was going on and on about a huge fucker and a pretty blonde. The guy tried to shoot him for trying to help the girl out with her form."

I crack a smile. "He was checking out my ass."

Lane and Dad stop laughing. "We need a new manager."

My mouth pops open in disbelief. "Dad, you can't be serious."

He gives me a look that says he *is* serious, and I touch his arm. "But, Dad, he was just looking."

"I don't give two fucks if he was looking or not. You're my daughter, and you are not an object to be stared at, especially by a stranger. Butcher should have shot him."

I throw my hands up in the air. This is crazy. Every one of them is fucking crazy. I think I am going to disown them. I huff and walk back into the living room.

Butcher is sitting on the floor, and Tiffany has his hand resting on the coffee table between them with a bottle of clear coat. "Quit moving and be a good boy. I will get you a cookie."

The look on Butcher's face does me in. I bend over, holding my stomach, laughing harder than I ever have in my entire life. This is the best thing I have ever seen.

"I think Auntie Shay has been drinking too much wine," Tiffany whispers to Butcher and I laugh harder. Gosh, I love that little girl.

I manage to control myself and I climb to my feet. Tiffany is done now and is putting the polish back in the drawer. Her back is to me. I sneak over to her, and I touch her sides, making her jump and spin around. I wrap her in a bear hug, her arms against her sides, trapping her as I smother her in kisses.

"Shay!" She screams with laughter, and I just continue pestering her face with kisses.

"Save me, Butcher!" she screams.

She is not fighting fair. I am lifted off the ground and I let her go, turn on Butcher, and start pestering his face with kisses.

"I will help you!" Tiffany yells a war cry and grabs my foot and starts tickling the bottom. I squeal with laughter and try to pull my foot away, but she holds on tightly.

"Uncle!" I scream with laughter.

She lets go and I take in deep breaths. "That'll teach you to mess with me!" she huffs, with her hands on her hips, and walks away from us. She is straight Lane's kid. There is no denying that.

"Let's eat, I am fucking starving."

I hear a loud and exaggerated gasp. "Grandpa! You cursed. You owe me ten bucks!" We walk in to see her standing in front of my dad with her hand out. My dad just smiles down at her like she is the cutest thing ever.

"It was an accident, your dad and aunt turned out okay."

She rolls her eyes and looks at me and Lane. "Okay is a word for it."

That little shit.

My dad throws his head back laughing, and I join in because she has Lane's mouth. Lane would always speak his mind. It didn't matter what it was—if he thought it, he said it.

"I am sure your dad curses all the time," my dad says.

"Not anymore. I've bled him dry."

Butcher laughs at that, and everyone looks over to watch him laugh.

"Hand it over, Pops." She holds her hand out again.

My dad rolls his eyes, reaches inside his pocket, and pulls out a ten.

"Thank you. This will go for my bra collection."

"Bras?" Lane says as he pales.

"Um, yeah Dad. Women wear those kinds of things." She looks at him like he is crazy and steps past him, pulls out a chair, and sits down. Poor Lane looks like he is about to pass out. Every girl at that age loves the idea of a bra. It's not a big thing.

"We going to eat or are you guys going to become a permanent part of the flooring?" I ask and start piling food on my plate and Tiffany's plate.

They all look at me and Lane gives me a look to kill. "I think you are rubbing off on my kid. She talks just like you."

I shrug. "So? She is awesome, and don't start with me—she has your mouth." I point my fork at him in warning.

Butcher pulls out a chair by my side and sits down. I grab his plate and fix his food for him, and I kiss his cheek.

"Do that again in front of me and I will duct tape your mouth closed," my dad tells me and I give him the middle finger.

"Dad, what does that mean?" Tiffany raises her middle finger showing Lane, who glares at me.

"See? Bad influence."

"Whatever." I grab my fork and dig into my food. It's silent as everyone eats. We all love our food and it shows. We don't speak a word as we feed our faces.

"Dad, can I go outside to play?" Tiffany asks and pushes her plate back.

"Sure, angel." He kisses the top of her head, and she slides out of her chair and runs outside. "Shay, want to go outside with her? I need to talk to Butcher." Lane's head snaps over to my dad. "About what I talked to you about earlier."

"Okay." I scoot my chair out and walk out the side door to the playground my dad built us when we were little.

Tiffany is swinging. "Hi, Shay. We need to go shopping again. My toes are getting chipped."

She is such a little diva. I love it. She puts her feet down and stops herself from swinging. "Come catch me!" she screams and runs out into the field. I laugh and follow in a slight jog.

She is a good thirty feet away when I see two dark shapes thrown over the fence. Two black dogs stand up and bark then take off in Tiffany's direction.

"Oh my god, Tiffany!" I run to her and the dogs are getting closer. She screams at the top of her lungs and runs in my direction. The dogs are ten feet from her now.

My heart is pounding so hard I can feel it up to my ears. The dogs are five feet away, and I sprint faster and grab my gun out of my holster. I put myself between Tiffany and the dogs. They are growling, foaming at the mouth, and huge.

One of them lunges and bites me on the calf. Its head shakes, tearing my skin. I scream for Tiffany. "Run!" The other dog charges for Tiffany. I click the safety off and shoot. The dog hits the ground—I shot it in the head. I don't want to kill dogs, but I will to protect Tiffany. The dog that had a hold of my calf lets go and lunges for my throat. I shoot again and it falls to the ground.

Three more dogs are thrown over the gate. I turn around and see Lane has Tiffany, Butcher is five feet away from me, and Dad is right on his heels. I try to walk and I fall to the ground.

"There are three more," I yell and Butcher and Dad raise their guns. Three shots ring out, and my dad runs into the field where the dogs were thrown over.

"Shay," Butcher chokes and falls to his knees beside me.

"I am okay," I reassure him and touch his face. He nods and looks over my body to make sure I am okay, and he spots the blood on my leg. He growls deep and loud. He grabs the bottom of my jeans and rips it up to my thigh. I can see the bite marks on my calf.

What if it has rabies or something else? I close my eyes as fear sinks in. Lips touch my forehead. "You will be okay, my Shay. I love you."

My heart stops right then and there. He just said he loved me. The pain is gone in an instant. I open my eyes and tears fall, because I know I love him too. "I love you too, Butcher," I whisper back and wrap my arms around his neck.

"Let's get you to the hospital." He picks me up bridal style.

My dad is running toward us. "I will take her, Butcher. Follow on your bike."

Butcher looks torn and I kiss him. "I will be fine."

He grinds his teeth before nodding.

I hear Tiffany crying and my heart breaks. She must be terrified. "Tiffany, I am fine, baby."

"You're hurt." Her eyes are on my calf.

I put on a brave face and wink. "It's just a scratch. This big oaf just wants to carry me." I will not let her bear the burden of guilt for me getting hurt. I would die for that little girl. Lane mouths to me, "Thank you."

If the dogs had managed to get to her, she would have been killed or seriously injured. Butcher hurries past Lane following my dad, who is running into his garage. I hear his truck start up and back out.

The passenger door is flung open, and Butcher sets me inside the truck. He kisses my temple. "Love you, Shay," he says in barely a whisper, so only I hear it.

God, I love this man. I just didn't realize how much until I almost died. He loves me too.

The door is slammed shut and my dad is off, speeding out of the driveway. He pushes the bottom of the dashboard to open the gate.

"Fuck! They threw dogs over the fucking gate." Dad slams his hand on the steering wheel.

"Dad, some things can't be stopped."

He shakes his head. "This isn't excusable, this will never happen again. You and Tiffany could have been killed."

Images flash across my mind. I can't imagine Tiffany getting hurt like that. These men knew our weakness, and that's why they threw the dogs over the gate.

"Dad, those dogs were heading straight for Tiffany. It's like they had her scent." I can hear the worry and pain in my voice. The adrenaline is wearing off, and I am feeling the dog bite.

"Lane is going to flip out." Nobody messes with his kid. This means war. "War," I whisper and Dad nods his head in agreement.

We pull up outside the emergency room. My door is flung open, and Butcher is waiting for me. His eyes are dark, and his mouth is clenched as he looks me over. I know it's tearing him up.

There are some things you can't control, and this is one of them. Who would have thought people would throw five dogs over a fence to kill someone? I hate the thought of those dogs being dead, but it was me and Tiffany or them.

That is not a chance I will take.

Butcher reaches in and scoops me out of my seat. I can feel the anger radiating off him. "Butcher, this is just a freak thing. You can't control everything. I am okay, I protected myself." I touch his cheek.

"I could have lost you. That is what is tearing me up inside. I need you like air," he mutters to me, and he steps through the emergency room door, carrying me in his arms.

A nurse comes over with a wheelchair. "What is wrong with her?"

"I was bitten by a dog," I tell her, and Butcher sets me down gently in the wheelchair. The nurse starts to push me away, and Butcher grabs my hand.

"I am not leaving her." He grips my hand tighter.

The nurse doesn't say a word, and I don't blame her. Butcher is a whole different level of scary right now.

I raise our entwined fingers and kiss the back of his hand, giving him comfort. I don't want him to be upset.

Butcher

Later That Night

She is never leaving our bed. Never again. I got the cuffs, and as soon as she gets her ass in my bed she is never leaving, her bakery be damned. I am going to have gray hair in the next month.

They threw dogs over the gate that were trained to kill, and it was Lane's daughter, Tiffany, who they went after. Shaylin put herself between her and the dogs. I am proud of her, but that doesn't mean I won't cuff her to my bed.

"Butcher?" Shaylin turns over, wincing as she rubs her leg against the bed. The bite isn't serious, but she did need a few stitches, which will have to be taken out in a week or so.

"Yeah?" I lean forward in my chair so I am face to face with her.

"I am ready to go home." It's 2:00 a.m. right now. They had to do a lot of testing to make sure the dog didn't have any diseases, and we just found out that they didn't.

"We are waiting on your prescription." I push her hair away from her face, and she closes her eyes. I can tell she is exhausted. I made her dad leave a couple of hours ago. He didn't want to, but I am with her and you couldn't force me to leave her side.

"When we get home, I could use some sex, but I don't feel like it. Maybe tomorrow?"

I lower my head and chuckle under my breath. She is out of it because of the pain medication.

"Anything you want, sweetheart."

She smiles at me widely before giving me a wink. Well, she squints one eye, and the other is halfway down. "You give good..." Her eyes widen as she dramatically looks around the room. "Orgasms." She gasps loudly and holds her chest. "Oh the crudeness I just spat out of my mouth." She says the last part in a British accent.

The doctor enters the room and hands me the prescription. "Well, I guess it's time for Shaylin to go home. She needs to go and get her stitches out in a week and get those antibiotics filled tomorrow. It's just an extra precaution. I hope you feel better, Shaylin." The doctor pats her shoulder.

She gasps loudly again and jumps away from him, her hand at her mouth. She looks at me in pure horror. "You just touched me!" She looks at me and leans closer to him. "You better run, or he will kick your ass."

The doctor looks at me, amused. "I bet he will."

Shaylin makes a shooing motion and he walks out. "Let's blow this weed." She puts her legs over the side of the bed. "Oh shoot...or was it 'let's blow this joint'?" She shrugs and makes a funny face. "Weed is weed. Joint is Joint. Bud is bud."

I laugh loudly and she raises her arms. "Carry me, Butcher. Carry me to your bed." I put one arm behind her back and the other under her knees, picking her up.

"I just love you, Butcher." She snuggles her head in my chest.

My heart beats a little faster. She loves me, this crazy fucker who thrives on violence.

I can say one thing though.

No one will love her as much as I do.

fifteen

Shaylin

One Month Later

"Butcher!" I screech and hold onto the headboard as he hammers into me. I love waking up in the mornings with his head between my legs and topping it off by fucking.

Perfect.

"Fucking sexy." He raises my legs so he can go deeper. and my legs shake.

"I'm so close," I moan and throw my head back, my toes curled to the heavens as I reach for the orgasm.

Then all of a sudden he slides off me, and I raise my head to look at him, giving him the death glare.

He chuckles and lies down on his belly, moving between my legs. He lowers his head and sucks my clit deep into his mouth while sliding two fingers inside of me.

"FUCK!" I scream and grab the back of his head, pulling at the strands. I explode and throw my head to the side. I feel Butcher moving then he slams inside me, which sets off another round of pleasure. A few seconds later he comes along with me, because every time he slides inside it feels like I am coming all over again.

He falls onto the bed beside me and I curl into him. "I do think you almost killed me that time." I feel his body shake with laughter, and my heart grows lighter.

His lips press into the side of my neck, and I shiver and move closer to him, still in his arms. "What time is it?"

"Ten."

I yawn and move closer, tucking my head into his neck, snuggling into his warmth. "I have to be at work at twelve. So let's squeeze in an hour nap?"

"We just woke up," he says, devoid of emotion.

I shrug. "The sex wore me out."

He chuckles and grabs the blanket, pulling it over both of us. His hand rests on the small of my back. I grab his free hand and twine our fingers together before pressing a kiss to the back of his hand.

I am not afraid to show Butcher affection—he loves it. Words are just words—you speak them, and they do mean something—but anyone can say words. It's actions that truly mean everything to him.

He drops me off at work before he heads to his clubhouse. Kyle and Lane have asked a few members to be on the lookout in their spare time until everything settles down again.

I was just bitten, but it could have been so much worse if I didn't have my gun on me. The people who want to funnel drugs through Lane's town are causing trouble, and they were the ones who threw the dogs over the fence.

I don't even want to know what Lane, Butcher, and Dad will do to them. It's none of my business. They can tell me whatever they want, but some stuff I am better off not knowing. They aren't saints—that is for sure.

"Hi Shaylin!" Paisley calls as I walk into the bakery. She is all smiles and glowing with happiness. Torch raised his daughter on his own, and he was a teenage dad. He did an amazing job with her.

"Hi Paisley, how are you today?" I step behind the counter and open the safe to stuff my purse inside.

"Liam sent me a letter today." She tries not to show it, but I can tell she is excited.

Liam saved her from a very bad situation. Since then they have become best friends, but I can tell that they are totally in love with each other from the letters and phone conversations and how she acts toward him. They aren't together though, and I think part of the reason for that is because he is a Navy SEAL and he is gone a lot. But I bet as soon as he is out, he is coming for her.

"How is it?" I smile at her, and her eyes are lit up with happiness.

"He is good, he is leaving for a mission soon." Her smile drops when she says "mission." I know she is scared for him.

"I am sure he will be okay." I pull her into a hug, and she hugs me back tightly.

"I can't help but worry about him. I know he is a badass and all, but he is not indestructible." I can see that this has been bothering her for a while. She lets me go and steps back.

"Nobody is."

She cracks a smile and wipes under her eyes. "Butcher probably is."

I laugh at that and walk back into the kitchen to make sure everything is ready for the cake delivery I have to make to a wedding in the next hour. They should have the cakes and cupcakes already baked, so I'll just have to ice them.

"The cakes and cupcakes are cool," my newest full-time worker informs me. Her name is Joslyn, and she is so shy around guys it hurts me. She can't even articulate a full sentence around any guy and Butcher, along with the other girls, thinks it's the cutest thing ever.

It really is cute and is why I fell in love with her. She is gorgeous and looks almost identical to Janna Kramer, but she doesn't realize how pretty she is. She is so shy, but she is an amazing baker, which is why I hired her immediately when she got out of school.

"Joslyn, you can help me if you want."

She smiles widely and begins icing the cupcakes in fluid motions.

For the next two hours, we work side by side decorating the cake and cupcakes. It was a big order, for a wedding of three hundred.

"You can come with me if you want to," I say once we have loaded everything up in the delivery truck.

One of the MC guys is staying here to watch over Paisley, and he is with another guy from the MC, who is second in command to Lane. His name is Wilder, and he reminds me a lot of Butcher. They are both quiet, and they are both people watchers and are super intense.

Plus I can't help but notice how he is staring at Joslyn like she is the best thing since sliced bread. I know she notices him too, because she has been one solid blush since the moment she saw him. Wilder is handsome, but not as much as my Butcher. Nobody can beat him, but Wilder is a close second.

"Okay." She hurries getting into the passenger side of vehicle. Wilder is staring her down.

I tap him on the shoulder, and he averts his gaze from her. "If you don't quit staring so hard, your eyes are going to fall out."

Wilder chuckles and rubs the top of my head. I consider Wilder a cousin—his dad was a member of the club before he retired, along with my father. There are a lot of boys who came from the first generation of the MC, and about twenty new members have arrived, along with three outsiders.

"She's gorgeous," he admits.

"She really is." I leave him standing there and climb in the driver's side of the delivery truck. I pull out of the parking lot with Wilder right behind me. I notice Joslyn staring out the window, watching him.

"So." I smile and glance over. As she looks at me, she knows she got caught.

"Yeah?" she practically whispers, her whole face red. She is so cute.

"You think Wilder is cute?".

"I think so, but he doesn't know I am alive. No man ever does, but I know for sure he doesn't. Look at him."

I snort and loudly. I see her cringe—she must think I am laughing at her. "Sweetheart, if you only knew what you actually look like. Wilder was just telling me before I got in the truck how gorgeous you are. You're beautiful, and you can pass for Janna Kramer's twin. Trust me, men notice you but you don't see them. I see them trying to approach you, but they don't got the balls."

Her mouth is open, and her eyes are wide as she stares at me in disbelief. What has her so down on herself? "I am?"

I give her a look that says she is crazy. "Yes, you are. Has no one ever told you how beautiful you are before?"

She shakes her head.

"Never?"

She shakes her head again.

"Fuck, that's dumb. Not even your family?"

"No, it was just my mom who I lived with, I have no other family. She always told me I wasn't pretty, and once guys never approached me, I guess I started believing it along the way."

My heart literally just broke, and now I want to go kick her mother's ass for saying such horrible things to her daughter. It's obvious that she is jealous of her.

"Well, I am sorry—she may be your mom, but she is stupid." I shake my head in anger. Some people are just horrible.

She bursts out laughing, and this is the first time I have ever seen her so happy. I am glad that I can put that smile on her face.

"Thank you, Shaylin," she whispers and I wink at her.

"Just telling the truth."

It's six o'clock and I am exhausted. The people at the wedding were snobby bitches who griped over everything. They didn't like how this one cupcake was sideways a bit, and the decoration on the bottom tier of the cake was slightly crooked. Once I could get away, Joslyn and I practically ran out the door.

Joslyn and Paisley should be back any minute from their break, and then Butcher will be here to pick me up for dinner.

Speak of the devil—I see Paisley and Joslyn outside my glass door. They open it and step outside. Paisley looks concerned about something.

"What is it?"

She points her thumb over her shoulder. "There are two people slumped over in the car outside."

My eyes widen and I run to the door then throw it open. I step out and I see it's Lexi's car. Her head is hanging down toward her lap, and the man's head is lying against the steering wheel.

Fuck me.

With hesitant steps I walk closer, and I feel Paisley at my back. I've got a bad feeling about this. I put one hand on my back, ready to pull my gun out at a moment's notice.

We are about five feet away and I hear a sharp cry, like a baby crying. The back window is tinted so we can't see inside. I split the distance to the car and put my head up against the window, cupping my hands around my eyes.

My stomach sinks at the sight. There is what seems to be a two-year-old baby sitting in a car seat that is falling over. It's a little girl. Her face is blood red, her clothes are stuck to her, and her dark brown curls are soaked.

The windows are rolled up and the car isn't on. She is burning up. I bang on Lexi's window, but she doesn't move. I scream, "Lexi!" She doesn't move and I pull the door handle, but it doesn't budge. Paisley is already on the other side of the car trying those doors.

All locked.

Looking around I see a large rock that I sometimes use to hold my door open. I run over and pick it up. I hear a motorcycle pulling up, but I don't look up—my mind is on getting the kid out of the car. She is going to die if I don't. It's one hundred degrees outside.

I step in front of Lexi's door, raise the rock above my head, and bring it down as hard as I can. Glass explodes everywhere, and I hear someone running up behind me.

"Shay?" Butcher yells. I reach inside and click the unlock button. I step back and pull the handle. The door opens and I reach inside, unbuckle the kid, and pull her from the seat.

"I called the police!" Joslyn yells.

The baby is hot to the touch, and she is completely soaked. My heart is breaking. She stops crying and lays her head on my chest, her little hands fisted in my shirt.

My heart just broke into a million little pieces.

"Shay?" Butcher says softly and I spin around.

"See if they are dead," I whisper and walk toward the bakery, wanting to get the baby out of the heat. Once we get inside, I sit down in the chair that Butcher usually sits in. "We got some water in the back. Grab me one along with a straw?" I ask Paisley. She runs off.

The little girl is wrapped around me like a monkey. "It's okay, angel." I soothe her and rock her from side to side. She loosens her grip slightly.

Paisley sets the water down on the counter.

"Thank you," I tell her and she nods sadly.

I take the water from the counter. "Drink, sweetheart." The bell above the door dings, and Butcher walks inside. He shakes his head, telling me what I already thought.

Lexi is dead.

The baby sits up shakily, and I put a hand at the small of her back. I raise the water to her and bend my head down so I can see her face. She reaches her little hands out, takes the water from me, and puts the straw in her mouth.

She drinks and drinks. Once she is done she hands it back to me, her little hands dirty. She then looks me directly in the face, and I fall in love right then and there. She has the most beautiful eyes in the whole world. They are large and such a light blue they look like ice.

Butcher walks around the counter and bends down so he is facing her. She studies him, and he just looks her straight in the eyes. She reaches her little arms forward.

She wants Butcher to hold her.

His eyes widen and he puts his hands under her arms, lifting her up. She lays her head on his chest. Butcher has a tortured look on his face, and I know I do too. She is breaking my heart.

I have so many questions! Why was she with Lexi? Is this little girl hers? I didn't know if she had a kid or not.

I hear the police sirens outside and I stand up. Butcher and I both walk outside, ready to face the music. Butcher stands to the side with the baby, and Paisley and I tell them exactly what happened.

The people from the ambulance check to make sure Lexi and the man are really dead and put them into body bags. "Here is the social worker. If we have any questions, I will call you." I nod and step back to Butcher, and the social worker walks up to us.

"Hi, I guess this is little Tiana?" The baby who we now know is Tiana raises her head to look at the social worker.

"Lexi was her mother?" I ask her.

She nods and her face saddens. "She was taken from her and was in foster care for a bit because of her mother being on drugs. Her mother just got her back six months ago. None of the mother's family would take her in, and their exact words were, 'I won't take in a drug baby.' So this little one will have to go back into foster care."

The social worker reaches to take Tiana, and the little girl starts screaming. She tries to crawl up Butcher's body and clutches his neck as tight as she can.

Butcher looks down at me and tears fill my eyes. "I can't," I say with a slight sob.

He nods. "We won't."

I can't let her go back to foster care. I just can't let her go through anything else. She is just a little baby, and she has never had a home to call her own. She has been given away from person to person. "We will take her."

The social worker shakes her head. "It doesn't work like that."

"I own this bakery, I have no record, and he is a Navy SEAL."

I point at Butcher, who pipes in. "No record—not even a ticket."

"Please let us keep her, we can give her a good home." I am ready to get on my knees to beg. Her little eyes are haunting me.

"There are proper channels," the social worker stutters.

"I will give you one hundred thousand dollars to make sure it goes through the proper channels and to get the adoption going as fast as possible," Butcher says. Thank God Butcher's role as a main member of the MC yields a generous share of the profits from their businesses.

Her mouth pops open, and I feel a hand on my shoulder. Looking up, I see Tiana reaching for me. I smile and take her from Butcher.

"I guess we can do that. Give me an hour to get the necessary paperwork, then I will help you through the proper channels. I also know a judge who will expedite everything. The adoption should be ready whenever you need it, for the right price."

"That isn't an issue. You have to sign a non-disclosure clause."

"Of course."

They are so corrupt, but right now I really don't care. I just couldn't bear the thought of letting her go. It feels like she is meant to be mine.

"Want me to go get Myra to come get you guys?" Paisley offers. "She has a car seat, and I am sure the baby needs to be checked out." I want to hug her right now.

"That would be amazing." What do kids need? We just have to go shopping tomorrow. "Do you think we can borrow some of Mia's clothes until we get her some tomorrow?"

"I can ask." Paisley steps away to make a call.

For the next hour I stand there as Butcher signs a bunch of paperwork. The car has been towed, the police are gone, and the ambulance is gone. It's just me, Paisley, Joslyn, and the social worker.

Myra pulls into the parking lot, and Ryan is right behind her. I guess they got a babysitter. Myra parks her car and steps out. The social worker recognizes her and greets her.

Butcher waves me over. "It's set and final. Just got to go to court," he whispers in my ear, and my heart lifts.

Tiana is fast asleep, and it's getting dark outside.

"I will speak to you tomorrow about what we talked about." The social worker gets into her car.

"Let's go home," I tell Butcher. He nods and kisses the top of my head before running his fingers through Tiana's damp curls.

Butcher

Shaylin buckles Tiana into the car and climbs in the passenger side. Tiana is two years old, and her birthday was yesterday.

I couldn't let her leave. She held onto me, crying for me not to let her go. I can't do that, not to some baby who has never had anything real her whole life.

Shaylin and I are going to have kids someday; we are just starting early. The sight of Shaylin pulling Tiana from the car fucking infuriated me. Then when I looked at her face for the first time, I saw pain and so much sadness.

I fucking ache.

When the social worker tried to say we couldn't take her, I resorted to fucking bribery. Tiana is mine, and I don't care what I have to do. If anyone in Lexi's family gave two shits, she wouldn't have been in foster care in the first place.

How can someone abandon their family? I lost all of mine in an instant, and I would do anything to bring them back. Some people just throw theirs away.

sixteen

Shaylin

I carry Tiana into the house, and my mind is going to a million different things right now. There are so many things we need to do.

Breathe, Shay, one thing at a time. I got this. The door opens and Butcher steps inside. He gives me that look that says everything will be okay. Tiana lifts her head from my shoulder and looks at Butcher.

"Want to set her on the bar here?"

I nod and carry her over to the bar. Myra has a bag open and set up on the bar. "I called the doctor. Tiana was seen six months ago. She is allergic to bees so I will write a prescription for an EpiPen. I have one extra here because Mia is also allergic." She reaches into the bag and hands me the EpiPen.

Butcher moves beside me. Tiana is staring around the room, and it's like I can feel her anxiety.

"Okay, sweetheart, I am going to put this on your chest, okay?" Myra holds up the end of the stethoscope. She doesn't say anything but allows Myra to do it. "Sounds good. Now I am going to check your ears."

For the next few minutes, Myra checks all of her vitals and looks in her mouth. She lifts her off the counter and puts her on the scale. "She is a bit underweight. So I would grab some

PediaSure to help bring it up. I don't think she has been getting the correct meals she needs."

I kind of figured that. Lexi is a selfish bitch. I hate that she is dead. Nobody should feel bad that Lexi is gone, but she has basically abandoned her baby girl. Tiana is underweight and looks like she hasn't had a bath in god knows how long. Her eyes are the most heartbreaking. They reveal her true feelings—she is so sad.

"I need to take her blood and make sure everything is what it needs to be."

I wince at the thought of her getting stuck with a needle, but it must be done. Myra grabs an alcohol pad and rubs her arm. When she pulls back, Tiana's skin is a lot paler than I thought—that is how much dirt is on her.

Butcher's hand clenches my hip, and I know he and I are looking at the same thing. Myra takes the butterfly needle and vial out. Tiana looks at the needle and starts screaming.

Butcher jumps into action. He picks her up and she curls into his arms.

My poor heart. I turn my head to the side to hide my tears. I can hear him whispering, "You are safe," in her ear. He sets her bottom on the bar top, but she holds her head to his chest, turned away from Myra. Butcher takes her arm and holds it out for Myra.

Myra walks over and quickly inserts the needle. I bend down so I am eye level with Tiana. I smile at her and run my finger over her cheek. She reaches out and wraps her little fingers around my index finger.

It hits me right in the feels.

"We brought a travel bed and some toiletries, along with some clothes, until you can go out tomorrow," Ryan tells us.

"Thank you so much, Ryan. This means a lot. Thank you also, Myra."

Myra smiles and pulls the needle from Tiana's arm. "It's what family is for. You would do the same."

Don't cry, Shay.

Myra puts the vials of blood in a small case. "I will tell you the results in the AM. We've got Alisha's mom babysitting."

"Thank you again." I slip my finger gently out of Tiana's grip and pull her into a hug.

"Everything will be okay, Shay," Myra whispers in my ear. She can feel my stress. I know everything will be okay. I just want to do right by Tiana. I want her to be happy.

Myra walks over to Ryan, who takes the bag from her. They walk to the door, and then they are gone.

Butcher and I look at each other. He is still holding Tiana.

"What do we do now?" I blurt out and he shrugs, but he smiles.

"I think a bath is a must?"

"Yeah, that is probably best and then I think she needs to eat."

Ryan sets the bags on the couch, and I walk over to see what they brought. They had clothes, diapers, sippy cups, shampoo, body wash, clothes, and underwear in case she is potty trained.

"Does she have a diaper on?" I ask Butcher and then, a second later, he says, "No."

I grab a nightgown, shampoo, bath toys, and body wash. "Let's do this."

Butcher lifts Tiana off the counter and places her on his hip. She lifts her head but holds onto his shirt for dear life. He follows me up the steps, through our bedroom, and into the bathroom.

I set everything on the shelf by the tub. "Butcher, want to get the bath water ready?" He lifts her to me and I set her down on her feet. She sucks her little hand and looks at me so sadly.

"Want to take a bath?"

She nods her head, and I smile widely at her because that's something. Right? I set the clothes on the counter and reach into the cabinets, grabbing some towels and washcloths.

I turn back around and undress her. I put my hands under her arms and set her in the tub. The water is still running, and she looks down at the bubbles around her. She scoops some up in her hand then, with her other hand, she touches it.

I get down on my knees and Butcher does the same. I lean over and kiss him on the cheek softly, and I run my hand down his back. His lips meet my temple and I close my eyes, sinking into his kiss.

Opening my eyes, I reach into the tub and scoop up a handful of bubbles. I peek at Butcher from the corner of my eye, raise my hand close to my mouth, and blow. The bubbles hit Butcher in the face.

He glares at me and a sharp peal of laughter pierces my ear. Butcher and I stare in awe. Tiana is grinning ear to ear as she watches me and Butcher. She blows the bubbles in her hand, and I jump in shock.

She laughs louder and does it again—this time to Butcher, who catches half of it before it hits him. She laughs harder, losing her breath this time.

"This is amazing," I whisper to Butcher as we watch Tiana enjoying herself playing with the toys in the tub, a wide smile on her face and, most of all, being carefree.

"She is amazing."

I wash her hair, and it's sickening the amount of dirt that comes out. It will take forever getting the tangles. Butcher comes back with a wide-toothed comb and starts brushing her hair.

I hide my smile at the sight of him being so gentle and caring. He gently brushes through every strand. He is so sweet. I pour a small amount of soap on a washcloth for her face. Being as gentle as I can, I wipe her face free of all the dirt and grime which makes her seem way tanner than she really is.

I take another cloth, which is barely wet, and wipe the suds away. I move down to her arms and hands then clean under her nails. I wipe her arms again, and that's when I see the bruises. I lift her arm. I can see a handprint, a bruise for every finger.

"What is it?" Butcher asks in a dark voice, and I show him her arm. Then I lift it, and I see another bruise on the back of the arm.

"Fuck." He clenches his jaw and shakes his head.

I wash the other arm and I see the same results. I stand her up to wash her legs, and I see her hips and backside are covered in bruises. She is two. There is no need to spank a child, especially hard enough to leave bruises like that.

"FUCK," Butcher hisses, and he stands up and walks out of the room. I hear something hitting the wall.

I finish washing her and grab the towel. She stands up, and I put the towel around her and lift her out of the tub. She shivers and I cuddle her close. I grab a second towel and dry her hair with it.

"Fank you."

Tears fill my eyes once again. My emotions are running high from everything that happened today. This little girl is affecting me in ways I never thought possible.

"You're welcome, angel." I kiss the top of her head.

I stand her up and grab the princess nightgown. Her eyes widen. "Pwincess."

"Yes, princess. You like it?"

She nods, and I know how I am going to decorate her room. I slip the gown over her head, and she pulls it away from her body so she can look down at it.

"Let's go downstairs."

She raises her hand for me to take, and my heart squeezes at the sight of her reaching for me. Together we walk down the stairs, going slow because of her small legs. She is so stinking cute in her nightgown.

Once we reach the bottom of the stairs, I am hit with the smell of something Butcher is cooking. My mouth waters because I am so hungry. We skipped dinner because of everything that went down.

I lead Tiana into the kitchen to see what Butcher is cooking. What do two-year-olds eat? I probably need to help him. So I take her into the living room and set her on the couch, and I turn on the TV and play some cartoons. She sucks her little finger and lays the back of her head on the couch. She is so stinking cute. Her hair is curling at the ends, and her eyes are to die for.

Leaving her alone on the couch, I can feel the worry gnawing on my stomach. She is just a few feet away. I repeat this over and over in my mind. When I step into the kitchen, Butcher turns around and then looks down.

"She is on the couch watching cartoons. What are you cooking? I am starving." My stomach growls in confirmation.

"Grilled chicken, steamed veggies?" he suggests and that sounds good to me.

"I can steam the veggies." I walk over to the cutting board and begin cutting the veggies.

We work together for the next twenty minutes, getting everything ready. I step out every few minutes or so to check on Tiana, and she is sitting in the exact same position.

We grab a small saucer and cup for her. I pour her some milk, and Butcher cuts her food into small pieces.

"I will go get her." I turn the corner to the living room, and she looks up as I walk in. "Food is done, sweetheart." She climbs down from the couch and takes my hand in hers. I lead her to the dining room. Butcher takes a stool that has sides and a back on it. It's higher than the dining room chairs. We don't have a booster seat.

Butcher has the plates and drinks set out. I bend down, pick Tiana up gently, and set her on the stool, then Butcher scoots it in. I sit down beside her, and Butcher sits on the other side. We both turn to watch Tiana. She reaches out slowly, takes a piece of chicken, and puts it in her mouth. She chews quickly, and she reaches out again, takes a handful, and starts cramming it in her mouth.

Butcher and I watch as she does this over and over until her whole plate is empty. We eat as we watch her. My heart is breaking seeing her so hungry. It's pretty obvious she hasn't eaten in a while.

"Butcher, I will get her some more."

He smiles softly and pushes Tiana's cup toward her.

I hurry into the kitchen, refill her plate, and cut her chicken into small pieces again. Once done I head back into the dining room, sit down beside her, and then scoot the plate back in front of her.

She reaches out immediately and starts eating. I go back to my food to finish it and Butcher does the same.

"Milk."

Butcher scoots his chair out and takes her empty milk cup into the kitchen. Tiana is gnawing on a piece of carrot. I smile at her and she ducks her head, smiling bashfully back at me.

She is so beautiful.

Butcher sets the cup in front of her and she smiles at him, just slightly but that is enough for him to grin at me.

Looking at the clock on the wall, I see it's nine o'clock. I take our empty plates into the kitchen and load them into the dishwasher.

Arms come up behind me, wrapping around my middle. I sink back into Butcher's arms, and he kisses my cheek. Sighing, I kiss the palm of his hand.

"I love you, Butcher, more than words can say."

He lets me go and spins me around in his arms. His fingers tug my chin, raising my head so I am looking into his face. "I love you too, my Shay."

I close my eyes and smile at the words. His Shay. I will never grow tired of him calling me that. I truly love him. I love him more every time he does sweet things, every time he surprises me—he is just Butcher. My Butcher.

Shaylin

Once Tiana is finished eating, I take her to the bathroom, and then we walk together into the living room. I am not sure how we'll get her to sleep—do I hold her? Rock her? Does she go to sleep on her own?

Butcher is sitting on the couch. He already set the little cot at the foot of our bed.

Tiana lets go of my hand as I sit down on the couch, and she raises her arms for me to pick her up. My stomach flips and I reach down and pull her up into my arms. She leans over and snuggles into my chest.

Butcher wraps his arm around my back and pulls me into his side. I lay my head on his shoulder and look up at him. He kisses me softly, his hand cupping the side of my face. He lets go suddenly and I look down. Tiana has wrapped her hand around Butcher's middle finger. She settles both of his hands behind her neck. She is using him to feel safe. She senses that he will protect her. I am glad that she isn't afraid to seek comfort in us. She reaches for both of us, and that alone is fucking amazing considering everything that she went through.

Tiana watches TV, and I cuddle with her and Butcher. I take the blanket off the back of the couch and cover her up once her eyes start to get heavy.

The show ends and I yawn. I look down and see she is fast asleep. "She is asleep."

"Want to take her?" He slips off the couch and I sit up. He lifts her out of my arms gently with her tucked against his chest, one arm under her bottom and the other on the top of her back. I pick up the blanket off the floor.

I follow Butcher as he walks up the stairs. He makes sure, as much as possible, that he doesn't jostle her. He steps inside the bedroom and over to the cot. It has rails on the side so she doesn't fall out. He has a thick blanket on top of the cot to make it softer. He gently lays her down on her back. I step up and cover her with the blanket from downstairs.

I yawn again and walk into the closet, and I grab a large shirt of Butcher's. I take off my clothes, including my bra, throwing them on the floor. I slip his T-shirt over my head and I groan. This is the best. I grab a pair of silk shorts and slip them on also.

Butcher steps inside, takes off his clothes, and puts on a pair of sweats.

When we enter the darkened bedroom, I peek down at Tiana and she is still asleep. I climb into bed and collapse, and Butcher slides in beside me.

"I forgot to take my makeup off." I could cry. My feet hurt and I am just drained.

Butcher slides off the bed and picks me up. "What are you doing?" I whisper, but he doesn't answer me. He carries me into the bathroom and sets me down on the counter. He reaches into a drawer and comes out with my makeup remover and the makeup pad. He lifts the bottle to read the directions.

He shakes it and then pours some out on the pad and brings it up to my face. I close my eyes as he wipes away all my makeup.

If I hadn't already fallen in love with him, I would have just then.

I hear him snap the bottle shut, and I open my eyes. He reaches behind my head. I feel him tugging on my ponytail, and my hair falls down my back.

"I love you," I blurt out, and he winks as he pulls out my hairbrush. He runs the brush through my hair, and I grab the waistband on his pants and pull him flush against me. I press my lips to his, and the brush clatters against the counter.

I pull back, but I am still face to face with him. "That little girl has stolen my heart. I can see so much hurt, Butcher. It makes me ache the way she ate her food like she hasn't eaten in a long time. No baby should feel that."

"I know, Shay, that's why I wouldn't let the social worker take her."

"She is Lexi's kid, Butcher, and Mary never mentioned anything. I could have gotten her."

He puts his finger on my mouth and gives me a fierce glare. "Don't say that, Shay, you couldn't have done anything. She is ours now. The before doesn't fucking matter, all I know is now. We are adopting that baby, then you're going to marry my ass. Cause you ain't fucking leaving."

Marrying his ass?

I watch in utter shock as Butcher reaches into a drawer beside the sink, and his hand comes out carrying a small box.

"Butcher," I whisper and I start to shake. This isn't what I think it is. Right?

He opens the box and I see a huge-ass diamond ring with a rose gold wedding band encrusted with diamonds and a large diamond on top surrounded by little ones.

Tears fall from my eyes and, when I look up at him, he smiles at me and his hand wipes away my tears. "Marry me, Shay, be my wife. Be mine. Forever."

"Yes!" I sob out. I raise my left hand, and he slips the ring on my finger. It fits perfectly. I throw my arms around his neck and pester his face with kisses.

He laughs and wraps both arms around my back, lifting me off the counter.

This is heaven.

He carries me out of the bathroom. "Let's get some sleep." He kisses the side of my head and I grin.

He doesn't let me go as he lies down on the bed. I slip off of him and settle my head on his chest. He settles his hand on my back. "Goodnight, Shay."

"Goodnight." I pinch his nipple. He jumps and his hand lands on my butt. I laugh quietly and close my eyes.

Butcher

I wake up with a jolt and look at the clock—it's 3:00 a.m. Something touches my hand, and I look down to see Tiana standing there looking at me.

"What's the matter?" I whisper and she raises her arms for me to pick her up. I reach down and pick her up, and I set her down on the bed. She crawls up beside me and lays her head on my chest. I grab the blanket and pull it over her. She puts her hand on my throat and cuddles closer.

My daughter. It hits me. I am going to be a father. No, I *am* a father. I grin and kiss the top of her head, and then I lean to kiss the top of Shay's.

My family. For the first time I have everything I never I thought I would have but dreamed I would.

seventeen

Shaylin

I wake up and see Tiana lying on Butcher's chest. My heart melts at the sight, and I slip out of bed and tiptoe out of the room.

I walk downstairs and gather the ingredients for pancakes. I make the batter, and then I take some bacon out of the fridge. I put it on and get busy making the pancakes.

Fifteen minutes later everything is done. I plate everything and begin the process of taking everything to the table. The jug of milk, three cups, three plates, and then the plates of food.

Once I am finished I hear a creak on the steps, and I see Butcher carrying Tiana, whose hair is sticking up everywhere.

"Smells good, baby." He kisses me and sets Tiana down in her seat. She rubs her little eyes and yawns.

I sit down and scoot my chair closer to Tiana to help her with her pancakes if she needs it. She takes her fork in her fist and stabs a piece of pancake, the plate rattling as she does so, then brings it up and puts it in her mouth.

"Butcher, we need to buy a car seat before we can leave to get Tiana everything for her room."

He nods and sets his fork down. "While you girls are getting ready, I will run out and get a car seat."

"Thank you." I blow him a kiss, and he shakes his head and goes back to his food.

I look at Tiana, who has abandoned her fork and is using her fingers to eat the pancake. She catches me looking and gives me a pancake-filled smile. I laugh and let her eat however she wants to—the fork is too big for her anyway.

We pull up outside a kids' department store. We are in Butcher's truck, so we will have plenty of room for everything because, basically, we have to start from scratch.

I step out of the truck, which earns a glare from Butcher since he told me to wait on him. Butcher opens the back door and unbuckles Tiana from her seat, then lifts her out and places her on her feet.

Tiana slips her little hand in mine, and Butcher takes my free hand. We walk through the parking lot, and Tiana jumps up on the sidewalk and bounces on her feet. I laugh at her goofiness.

Butcher opens the door for us, and we step through the entrance. Tiana takes her hand from mine and grabs the sides of her little dress, twisting it as she walks in front of us. I love that she is letting loose more and more with us.

Butcher puts his hand on the small of my back as we follow her through the store. Tiana checks out everything she comes across, and she makes a beeline straight to the toy aisle ahead of us.

Butcher and I speed up to catch up to her. Tiana grabs a stuffed kitty and hugs her to her chest then swings from side to side. I bend down next to her. "Do you know what this is?" I touch the kitty's head.

"Titty."

I suck my lips in my mouth so I won't laugh, but Butcher doesn't care enough to hold it in. He laughs behind me.

Someone left a shopping cart and I pull it over to us, lift Tiana, and put her in the front part of the basket. She is still holding on to the kitty. As we go down the aisle, she points at some things she likes and we get them for her, because she literally has no toys at all.

Thirty minutes later we leave the toy aisle and head to the furniture section. I immediately spot a bed that is light pink, with princess crowns on the poles on every corner of the bed. The sides are pink, and the top is skimmed in gold. They have a dresser, vanity, toy chest, lamp, nightlight, curtains, and everything we need for the room, right down to blankets, pillows, and bean bag chairs. Perfect.

"Hi, how can I help you?" A worker pops out of nowhere, and Tiana and I both jump. Butcher growls loudly and moves around us to face the worker. "Do you deliver?"

She nods and smiles, all too chipper for my liking. Why is she looking at Butcher like that? Hell, no.

"Well, we would like the bedroom suite here." I point to the princess room.

She nods and moves to a computer. "Would you like it delivered today and set up?"

I look at Butcher and he nods. "Yes, that would be perfect."

"Would you like to go to your dad's while we get everything set up? I think your dad needs to know, and I got a call when I was out today to get the car seat. We got to go in and sign some papers—then she is ours."

"I can't wait." I smile and kiss the top of her head.

I step around the buggy to the counter, and I hand my credit card to the worker before Butcher can do anything about it.

"Shaylin," he growls and I laugh.

Honestly, I am not hard up for money. My bakery is doing very well, plus I am a trust fund kid. I have barely touched my trust fund. I rented my house out and used it to buy my bakery, along with all of my equipment.

"I will let you buy the clothes and toys."

He gives me a death glare and I wink. He gives me that look that says I am getting it later, not that I mind. I missed him last night, if you know what I mean.

My ring catches the light, and my stomach flips because it's so surreal that I am going to be getting married.

"Is that all for you, ma'am?" I take my card from her outstretched hand. "That's it. Thank you." I take my receipt.

"Fill out this form with your address, so they can deliver. They should be there in three hours," she tells us.

Butcher steps up and fills out the form, and I see her watching his every move. I glare at her. She looks at me, and I cock my head to the side and arch my eyebrows at her, letting her know she is caught.

She looks down at the ground and turns to Tiana, who is holding her stuffed animals.

"You like them?" I ask and place a stray hair behind her ear. She nods and hugs the stuffed animals under her neck.

"Ready, baby?" Butcher says and I look up from Tiana.

"Yeah."

He takes the buggy from me and pushes it toward the clothes department. I turn to look at the worker, who is staring at us. I smirk and scoot up next to Butcher, and I reach down and grab his butt.

I hear her gasp and I laugh.

"Someone is being naughty," Butcher teases and I give him a look.

"You love it."

He doesn't say anything, but I know he does because I love it when he gets all possessive.

From the clothes that Myra sent, I know Tiara's size. Butcher stays outside the kids' clothes section with Tiana. I comb through the clothes, getting dressy clothes, pajamas, socks, undies, play clothes, a bathing suit, hair bows, and everything else I can possibly think of. I get an armload and drop it in the buggy.

An hour later I am finished. I can always come back and get whatever else we need. I drop the last load.

"We need to go to Walmart next to get other things she needs." We have an hour before Butcher needs to go back to the house to meet the delivery people.

We arrive back at his house fifteen minutes before we need to. Walmart was hell. We had to get shampoo, toothpaste, cups, plates, forks, meds, a booster seat, brushes, and lotion. Then Butcher found the snack section for toddlers, and he insisted that we load up on that because it's good for her.

Gotta love that man.

We put Tiana on the couch with some toys as I help Butcher load all of the stuff into the house, at my insistence. He wanted me to relax with Tiana, but I wouldn't. I dread hanging up all the clothes tonight once I get home from Dad's.

I wonder how he will react once he finds out that Butcher and I are adopting Tiana. You know what? I am not going to worry about it, because once he sees her he is going to fall in love.

Paisley and Joslyn are running the bakery for me today, and they are a godsend at times like this, but I need to find a babysitter who can watch Tiana when Butcher and I are working. Butcher's schedule is lenient though.

"That's all of it." I dust my hands and wrap my arms around Butcher's middle. He kisses the top of my head and runs his hand up and down my back. I sigh and close my eyes.

"Call me once you get to your dad's?" he asks and I nod then pull out of his arms.

"I will. Love you." I rise on my tiptoes and kiss him chastely, but he digs his hands in my hair and pulls me hard against him, deepening the kiss.

I smack his ass hard and he bites my lip. "Promise for later?" I ask.

His answer is his signature smirk.

"Tiana, come here angel!" I hear her little feet hitting the hardwood floor. She pops around the corner, and I smile because she is carrying the stuffed kitty under her arm.

I open one of the Walmart bags and take out a couple of snacks, along with some juice boxes. She steps up next to me, and I take her free hand. Butcher opens the front door, and I reach behind my back to make sure I have my gun.

"Love you," I call over my shoulder as I walk to my car.

"Love you more."

I rub my chest and open the back door to the car. Tiana steps inside and climbs into her car seat, and I lean in and buckle her in. I open her juice for her and set it in the cup holder and then open some snacks. I set the pack in the cup holder.

I slide out and shut the door, and I wave up at Butcher, who is watching us. He is too hot, standing there all broody like.

The gate is already open, thanks to Butcher, and it shuts after I drive out. I click the button on the steering wheel. "Call Dad."

The phone rings a couple of times before he picks up. "Hey, baby girl."

"Dad, I will be there in forty minutes—is that okay?"

He laughs. "Of course it is. See you in a bit." I click the button again to end the phone call.

I arrive at Dad's forty minutes later, and that's when the nerves kick in. I have two bombshells. One, I am engaged and two, I am adopting Tiana.

Oh boy.

I park the car and I take a couple of deep breaths, controlling myself. He steps out onto the porch, and I see him scoping out the yard, my guess is to check for dogs.

Oh my god, I repeat over and over in my head.

You can do this.

I pop open my door and wave at him. He smiles at me and I smile back. I turn my back to him and then open the door behind me. I reach inside and unbuckle Tiana, and she climbs out, then steps out of the car.

I shut the door, and I see a million different emotions come across my father's face in one split second. I lick my now-too-dry lips. Tiana has her stuffed kitty under her arm.

"What is going on, Shay?" Dad asks and I shake my head. I won't do this in front of her. When we are in the house, I lead her straight to the living room. "Play with your toy in here, okay? I will be right in here." I point toward the kitchen. She climbs on the couch and starts playing with her new toy.

I step into the kitchen, and my dad is already sitting at the table, giving me that signature Smiley glare. I pull out my chair and sit down facing him.

"Butcher and I are adopting Tiana," I begin. Then I tell him everything that happened. I tell him every detail, including Butcher paying the social worker.

"Shay, you did the right thing," he says, and I am instantly relieved because I just wanted his approval.

"She stole my heart, and Butcher was ready to rip everyone apart who dared to take her from him. She affected us both."

Dad gives me a pointed look. "Little girls do that to you."

I laugh and run my hand over my face.

"So he finally got that ring on your finger?"

My eyes widen and I wince on the inside.

"Shay, he already asked me and I don't think anyone is good enough for you, but I do know Butcher is gone for you."

"I love him, Dad, I really do."

Dad smiles at me softly. "I know you do, Smiles." His smile drops. "If he fucks up, he is dead."

I laugh and I hear little footsteps. Tiana crosses the room and stands by me, and she looks at my dad with wide, curious eyes.

"Fuck, Shay, her eyes."

"I know."

Her eyes are something else; that's for sure. They are beautiful.

Dad lifts his hands toward her, and she looks at him, unsure, for a few seconds before lifting her arms for him to pick her up. He puts her in his lap. They stay like this for an hour, until she falls asleep in his arms, and I fall more in love with her by the second. Everything she does I find amazing.

"Shay, she has already taken my heart," Dad informs me and I knew it would happen.

"I know how you feel, Dad." I run my finger up her cheek.

"I wish you was a baby again, Shay, you grew up too fast."

"Aww, Dad." I kiss his cheek and lay my head on his shoulder. I love my dad. He was always my best friend growing up. He, Lane, and I were best friends. We spent every weekend together. We went camping, fishing—whatever we were up for.

My phone buzzes in my pocket, and I take it out.

Butcher: Everything is done.

Me: Leaving now.

"Dad, I am going to head home. It's been a long day. Would you mind carrying her out for me?"

He gives me a look telling me he doesn't fucking mind, and I don't ask again. I know my dad like the back of my hand.

I step out of the house, and Dad follows me. I open the back door, and Dad sets her gently in the car seat, without waking her up, then buckles her in.

"Bye, Smiles." He hugs me and I hug him back. "Bye, Dad."

I climb in and gently shut the door so I don't wake her. I text Butcher that I am pulling out of the driveway and start the car.

eighteen

Shaylin

"Potty." I jolt at the sound of Tiana's voice in the backseat. I didn't know she was awake yet.

We are just outside of town, and there is a gas station right up ahead. I take her inside to do her business. In and out quickly, and I am ready to go home to my man and to pull this bra off.

"You ready to go home? We have a big surprise for you!" I tickle under her chin and she lets out a peal of laughter. I take out my phone and shoot a text to Butcher, **"We are leaving now, Butcher."**

Something wraps around my hair, and I am pulled out of the backseat. My phone skids across the parking lot. I fall and the side of my head hits the ground hard.

Tiana!

I see a man in the backseat of the car, and Tiana is screaming. I scramble up and grab him by his hair. I pull with all of my might, yank him out of my car, and push him onto the ground. I see a man running toward me.

I do what I am known for: I smile.

I reach behind me and take out my gun, cock it, and point it at the man running toward me, and I shoot his right knee out. He falls to the ground screaming.

Something hard hits me on the side of my face, and I spin around. The fucker just punched me. I grin at him. He stumbles, and I pull back my fist and nail him in the face. I do this over and over again. He hits the ground, and I stomp on his dick.

"Fucked with the wrong person, fucker!" I scream and bring up my gun. I shoot one hand, then the other, and then his knee so he can't get up.

His screams of agony make me smile wider. I stalk over to the man who was running toward me. He has a gun, and I shoot it out of his hand. He tries to stand up, but I wrap my hand around his hair and slam his face on the ground. I do this over and over again.

"Who the fuck do you work for?" I ask him.

He makes a gurgling sound. "Her father." I smash his face one last time and run back to the car. The MC will clean up this mess.

My blood runs cold at him saying "her father." He is after Tiana. I spot my phone and pick it up. I see it's shattered. I stuff it in my pocket, run to the car, and open the back door to check on Tiana.

She is screaming at the top of her lungs, and I see she is still buckled in. "I am okay, angel. You're safe," I soothe her and she immediately stops screaming and holds her kitty tighter. I kiss her forehead and she grabs a hold of my ear.

I gently remove her hand from my ear, and I feel blood running down my face. I shut the door and kick the fucker in the head again because he is awake now. I get back into the car and throw it into reverse, shoot out of the parking lot, and speed away toward the clubhouse.

A minute from the scene, I meet Butcher's MC members. I stop right in the middle of the road and roll down my windows, and they do the same. "Get those two fuckers at the scene, all right?"

Locke and Techy stare at me in horror. I roll up my window and I meet more members, but they follow me back to the club. I pull through the gates and park the car. I am surrounded by people. The MC members pile off their bikes, and women run out of the clubhouse. My door is wrenched open, and I am pulled out.

"What happened?" Kyle holds my face in his hands, but I throw them off and open the back door to unbuckle Tiana and take her from her seat. She curls into my arms.

"I will explain inside. Tell Butcher that I am safe?"

Kyle gives me an appraising look. "He knows. He is twenty minutes out."

"Let's go." I am not taking any chances with my daughter. An assload of people are following me inside the clubhouse, but I go straight back to the room where they have their meetings.

I sit down in a chair, and someone hands me a blanket for Tiana. I tuck it around her, and I feel her body relax.

I am so fucking pissed right now. Someone tried to take my kid.

The door shuts and I start from the beginning, telling them exactly what I did to those men. "They are after Tiana. Those men are still fucking alive, and I want a piece of them once you bring them here. I left all the vital stuff intact."

Kyle cracks a smile, and the guys around the room start laughing.

"You're perfect for Butcher."

I look down at Tiana and see she is looking up at me. "He will be here soon."

"SHAYLIN!" he roars and the door is ripped off its hinges and thrown in the hallway.

He calms down when he sees me, but he takes in the cut on my forehead. "Who are they? They are so fucking dead." Tiana climbs out of my arms and runs to Butcher. He picks her up, and she stuffs her face in the side of his neck.

"Get your ass over here, Shay." I stand up and fall into his arms. Safety. My body slackens. I didn't even know I was shaking so hard.

"They were after Tiana, her dad."

He stiffens.

"Dude, you should fucking see these men. This chick fucking beat the shit out of them. The worker in the gas station said she done it smiling."

I feel Butcher shaking with laughter.

What can I do? I am my father's kid.

Butcher

The fucking fear at hearing about her getting attacked will never leave me. I thought my world itself had ended.

Thank fuck Shaylin knew what to do and she can protect herself. If she didn't have that gun, shit, it would have been bad. I felt so fucking helpless, because I was thirty minutes out.

I am proud of her—she protected herself and Tiana. She did what she had to do—and she got the job done—but I wish it never came to that.

I listen as Kyle relays everything that went down. Shaylin is pressed hard against me, and Tiana is asleep on my chest.

"They are in the back room."

"Let's have some fun."

"I want to come." Shaylin grabs my arm, and I study her face. Is she up for that? Most of the women don't join in, but they are fucking with our kid—that's a whole different thing.

"You sure?"

She grins at me, giving me all the answer we need. I stand up and place my hand on Tiana's back so she doesn't stir awake.

Shaylin

We walk into the main room, which looks like a huge living room. A woman who is gorgeous and can pass as Alisha's twin stands up off the couch. She has strawberry blonde hair and large doe eyes like Alisha. I think this is Alisha's mom.

"Is Myra here?" I ask her and she shakes her head.

"I can watch her, I watch Mia for Myra."

I look at Butcher and he nods. She smiles at me and reaches her arms out for Tiana. Butcher settles her into her arms, and my stomach sinks at the thought of leaving her after everything that went down.

I want answers.

Butcher takes my hand and leads me to a side room. He shuts the door and grips my face in his hands. "Sweetheart, I don't want this to fuck with your mind. I am someone you have never seen before in there. I don't want your view of me to change."

"That is not possible, Butcher. We all have different parts of ourselves. I am going in there to make them fucking pay for trying to kidnap Tiana, then I want to rid this earth of her father."

Butcher stares into my eyes before he shakes his head and kisses me on the forehead. "I love you, my Shay."

My heart flutters and I wrap him in my arms and hug him tightly to me.

"Let's go show them what crazy is."

I erupt into laughter because we are out of the norm, but normal is overrated. Love is not normal—love is something wild and untamed. What I have with Butcher is something different altogether—it's all-consuming.

"Let's do this."

We step out of the storage room and, hand in hand, we walk back to the room where the men are held. I made sure they weren't seriously injured for this very reason.

Nobody fucks with my kid.

Butcher opens the door and we step inside. Everyone is already there. The men are awake, and they are hanging from the wall by chains, their feet barely touching the ground. Their eyes widen as they see me then move to Butcher, who is holding my hand.

Something dark stains the one whose face I beat into the ground. "He just pissed his pants." I look at Butcher, amused, and I see he has a knife out, slicing it across the man's face.

Well, that will do it.

Butcher lets go of my hand and steps toward the men, and I move over to stand next to Kyle. He looks at me, unsure. "You sure you're up for this?"

I roll my eyes. "I am not Butcher's woman for no reason, plus look at my dad."

Kyle laughs and gives me a knowing look. "Touché."

Butcher stops in front of them. "You attacked my woman and tried to kidnap my kid. Do you know what that means?" I shiver at the sound of Butcher's voice. He is a different Butcher right now.

"She isn't your kid."

I see Butcher's body stiffen, and his hand shoots out. A knife is embedded into the man's shoulder blade. "Death. You're going to die. Both of you, but you can die a painful death or we can drag it out for days. Your choice. You be good little fuckers and answer my questions."

"Now, who wants Tiana?" Butcher takes the knife out of the man's shoulder, and he screams loudly.

"Her father. Levi Barnes."

"The fucking drug dealer?" Techy pipes in.

The man nods.

"Why does he want her?" Butcher nicks him right under his neck.

"I don't know. I just got paid to kill her and take the kid." He looks at me.

Butcher growls loudly, raises his hand, and embeds the knife in the top of his head. His head rolls to the side—he is dead. Butcher roars loudly and stalks to the other man. "Do we need anything else from these fuckers?" Butcher asks.

"No," Kyle answers him.

"They don't deserve to breathe another breath that my Shay breathes." He takes the knife from the man's head and turns to the other guy. He drags the knife down his chest and then up through the bottom of his throat and up to his brain. Dead.

"Let's go track down this Levi. Got an address, Techy?"

"Already got it," he says and Butcher walks to me. "Take Tiana home? Your dad should be here any minute, and he is to stay with you. I am ending this."

I nod and kiss him hard. "Come back to me in one piece. Yeah?"

He nods and cups the back of my neck. "Anything for you."

We walk into the mail room, where Tiana is. I need to get her home and calmed down.

My eyes go to Tiana, who is sitting on the floor with Adeline. Tiana is smiling gleefully, playing with some toys. I let out a deep breath of relief. I do believe I need to hire her to watch Tiana for me once I go back to work.

The door slams open, and my dad charges in with Lane. Dad looks at me and pulls me into him hard. "Fuck, Shaylin, I am going to have a heart attack! Are you okay? Tiana?"

"I am fine, Tiana is fine."

He nods and hugs me tighter to him.

"We need to roll out, Butcher," Kyle calls and Butcher, with his eyes on Tiana, looks like he doesn't want to go.

"We will be waiting at home for you." He nods and steps out of the room, and I can see he is fighting himself with every step.

Dad lets me go and leaves the room. I pull out of his arms, and I reach down and pick Tiana up. Adeline gives me a soft smile. "She is such a sweet child. I will watch her anytime."

Tiana is running her hands through my hair.

"Actually, I wanted to talk to you about that. I have to go back to work in a week or so."

"Call me and let me know." She stands up and I am struck again by how pretty she is.

I stand beside the couch. My dad is walking toward me while looking at his phone. "Shaylin, my truck is right outside."

"Okay."

He looks up from his phone at Adeline. He stumbles and I jolt. What the heck? He looks at me and gives me a huge-ass smile. Then he looks back at Adeline, who is blushing. He moves past me and stops right in front of her. "I am taking you out tonight."

My jaw hits the floor.

He reaches behind her and takes her phone out of her pocket. He types something and then his phone is ringing. "Text me your address, gorgeous."

What the fuck?

Adeline's mouth opens and closes multiple times before she nods. He gives her his signature smile and steps away from her. "I will be at the truck, Shaylin."

Well, I will be damned!

Adeline stares at me wide eyed. "What happened?"

I have no answer for that but, "You just got Smileyed."

She sits down on the couch, and I laugh because I would be confused myself. I walk outside, and Dad takes Tiana from me and puts her into her car seat. I climb into the passenger side, and a minute later Dad joins me.

He catches me staring at him, and he looks at me then back out the windshield. "What?"

I grin and cross my arms across my chest. "I didn't know you were so smooth."

He chuckles and winks at me.

My dad hasn't dated in a very long time, and what changed? Adeline is gorgeous, and you can see the happiness that radiates off of her—that's why I want her to watch Tiana.

"She is very pretty," I pipe in.

"She's fucking hot."

I put my hands over my ears. "No more, Dad."

He bursts out laughing.

I shake my head and look in the backseat at Tiana, who is playing with her toy. She looks so calm, and it's crazy how much a kid can bounce back from.

Dad pulls over and into a drive through at a local pizza place. Thank goodness. I am starving, and I know Tiana is getting hungry also.

Dad hands me the box of pizza, and I tear a small slice into pieces. I hand Tiana a piece, and she immediately places it in her mouth. I take a juice box out of my purse, put the straw in, and place it in her cup holder.

For the next forty minutes, I hand her small bites and I stuff my face in between. Dad basically eats half of the pizza himself.

We pull up outside of Butcher's, and I tell him the code. The gate opens and then slams closed once we get a few feet away from it. It's sensor automated.

"Where is his house?" Dad asks.

"Right across this bend."

Just as I said, it pops into view—just as breathtaking as the first time I saw it. "Nice house."

"It is."

"You always wanted to live in this kind of house when you were little. You talked about marrying and living in a log mansion."

I snort, because it's true. This house was my dream house. "How ironic," Dad says and I nod.

He pulls to a stop, and he climbs out and takes Tiana from the backseat. What I want right now it is to veg out on the couch. I take out my phone and see it's just five o'clock. I think a nap is in order, and I know Tiana is tired. She started to fall asleep once we got close to Butcher's.

I walk up first, put in my key, and step inside. I disarm the alarm and click everything to arm the gates so someone can't climb over them. Dad puts Tiana down and shuts the door. I click the button on the iPad, locking every door in the house and alarming all of the windows.

"When did he get all of this installed?" Dad has similar security in his house.

"Right after we got together. Let's go get changed," I tell Tiana and she takes my hand.

Her room is done! I totally forgot about it. I can't wait to see her face. I lead her up the stairs and into the bedroom that is straight across from ours. I push the door open and I gasp.

It's gorgeous, and all of her toys have been opened and are lying on the toy chest. Her bed is put together, the bed made. I walk over to her chest, and I see her pajamas are already folded. I walk to the closet and see everything is already hanging.

Thank goodness.

Tiana squeals with laughter, and she crawls to the top of her bed, grabs a pillow, and laughs. She stands up, jumps, and falls back on the bed. She does this for a good five minutes while holding her pillows.

She loves it.

I take out a new nightgown for her and walk over to the bed. I reach for her and she jumps off the bed into my arms. I tickle her sides and she laughs louder.

God I love this little girl.

I change her and help her off the bed. I grab one of the throw blankets we bought her this morning. She walks in front of me downstairs, and seeing her being so independent brings on a rash of different emotions.

She steps off the last step and takes off running into the living room. I hurry after her, and she is already plopped down on the couch next to Dad.

This little girl destroys hearts everywhere she goes. I hand Dad the blanket and he covers her up, and she settles her head against the side of his chest.

I sit down next to her and rest my head on the back of the couch. I am just drained, and I've got a massive headache where I clipped my head on the pavement, plus I was punched. My head scraped the ground, and that is why it was bleeding.

I wonder what Butcher is doing right now?

Butcher

I kick in the motherfucking door at the house where the drug dealer lives. Three men jump off the couch and point their guns at me. I raise my gun and nail two of them, and Techy gets the other. I stalk farther into the house, Techy by my side and the others bringing up the rear.

When I walk into the kitchen, I am face to face with Levi. "Just the man I was looking for." I wrap my hand around his throat. Shots are fired around me, but my eyes don't leave the man who had my woman attacked and tried to take my kid.

"What do you mean?" Levi starts sweating, and he is looking at everything but me.

I drag him from the kitchen to the living room. "You know who the fuck I am." I toss him on the ground, and he gets up to his knees. "Look me in the eyes, I want to be the last fucking thing you see. The man who killed you and sent you to hell. You attacked my woman and tried to kidnap *my* daughter." When I say "my daughter," he looks at me with narrowed eyes. "Yes, my daughter. I am going to be the father she fucking deserves and protect her from sorry fuckers like you."

"I love Tiana."

Rage fills me at the sound of him saying her name. "No, you don't." I raise my gun and pull the trigger, and he slumps over to the ground.

It's over. No more ties to Tiana.

Kyle touches my shoulder. "Go home to your family. Shaylin needs you."

I nod and walk out of the house. They will clean everything up, and it will be like nothing ever happened.

Let's go home.

nineteen

Butcher

Smiley meets me at the door. He nods for me to walk into the kitchen and I follow him, but all I want right now is to be in there with my fucking woman.

"Is it done?" he asks.

"Levi is dead and a lot of his crew."

Smiley nods. "I got a date to go on. See you later."

"Date?" I ask.

He smirks at me. "Adeline."

He shuts the door behind him, and I rearm the door and gates once he has left the property. I walk into the living room, and I see Shaylin and Tiana asleep on the couch. I squat down in front of Shaylin and kiss her lips softly. Her eyes flutter open and she smiles a slow smile. She lifts her hand out of her blanket and places it on my cheek.

God I fucking love her.

"What time is it?" She asks and yawns.

"Seven."

"I will go whip up some spaghetti." She kisses me before placing her lips next to my ear. "Tonight, you are mine."

"Can't wait." I pull her hair and she shoots me a fiery smile.

Shaylin

Butcher takes out a plate for Tiana and cuts up her spaghetti, and I pour her some milk. Our food is already at the table, and Tiana is sitting in her new seat. I put the garlic bread on the table, and Butcher places Tiana's plate in front of her along with her drink. She takes her little spoon and spoons up some spaghetti, getting it all over herself. I laugh and wipe her mouth off then hand her a piece of garlic bread.

"This is delicious, my Shay." My stomach flutters at him calling me "my Shay." I love hearing him calling me that. I love him so much.

"Do you know how much I love you?" I ask.

He shakes his head and gives me a teasing look.

"The thought of losing you makes it hard to breathe, if you did leave I wouldn't survive. You are what I think of when I first wake up and the last thing at night."

"Shay," he whispers and he swallows hard. I know he wants to say so much, but he doesn't have to.

"I know, Butcher."

Tiana is sound asleep. We laid her in her bed and told her a story, and she was out. Now it's time for me and Butcher.

Butcher shuts our door, locks it, and begins pulling off my clothes. My body is on edge with anticipation.

Once I am completely naked in front of him, he walks behind me, pushes my hair over my shoulder, and kisses the back of my neck. Goose bumps spread down my back. His lips move to my shoulders and I shiver.

"Bed."

I climb on the bed, and Butcher strips out of his clothes and climbs into bed with me. I lean forward and kiss him. He tucks his hand in my hair, not allowing me to move—he is taking control.

I run my hand down his side and wrap my hand around him. He growls deeply and smacks the side of my ass. I jolt and grow wetter. The hand that smacked the side of my ass moves over to my pussy and slides two fingers inside, curling his fingers until he finds the spot.

The spot that drives me crazy.

I pull my mouth from his, throwing my head back, gasping. His lips wrap around my nipple and he sucks deep.

"Oh." I moan and twine my fingers in his hair, pulling at the ends. His thumb rubs my clit, and my body stiffens.

I gasp in shock as I am flipped onto my front, face down on the bed and ass up in the air. His dick touches my entrance, and I grab the sheets for leverage.

He slams inside hard, my hips leaving the bed. I cry out, my eyes closed tightly as pleasure hits me and I come. He keeps on pounding inside of me, and my breath is coming out in short pants.

I push myself back against him and he smacks my ass. I clench around him and throw my hair back over my shoulder.

"Still."

I shudder at his command, not that I would listen. I press myself harder this time, and he goes deeper than ever before. My head hits the bed, my whole body shaking and seized up as I come again.

"Ah Butcher," I hiss and my body collapses on the bed. I feel him coming inside me a second later.

He falls to the side and takes me with him, my head on his shoulder. "I think I will pass out now," I mutter.

He climbs out of bed and my head rolls to the side. A minute or so later, he comes back and I crack open my tired eyes. I see him with a first aid kit, makeup removers, and a brush. He opens the first aid kit and takes out a cleaning cloth. I close my eyes, and he pushes my hair over to the side and tilts my head slightly so he has better access.

He cleans the wound, and I make sure not to wince so Butcher doesn't get worked up. I learned a long time ago not to show that I am hurt because it messes with him.

He shuts the first aid kit and opens my makeup remover and puts it on a cotton ball.

This is why his actions show so much more than his words ever would. Everyone deserves a Butcher, someone who will take off their makeup for them if they are tired and brush their hair. I have never felt so loved and cherished in my whole life.

After he cleans my face he sits behind me, his legs on either side of me, and brushes my hair free of tangles. It takes everything in me not to sob like a little baby. This is Butcher showing me what I mean to him. I am so fucking blessed.

twenty

Shaylin

It's official. Tiana is ours. We just signed the papers and everything is final. A weight has been lifted off my shoulders because nobody can try to take her away—she is ours.

Butcher is taking Tiana home, where Adeline is going to watch her as I work today. I have to go back, and it's killing me leaving her, but she will be perfectly fine with Adeline.

I walk into the bakery, and I am greeted by Joslyn. She pulls me into a hug, surprising me.

"I am guessing you missed me?"

She laughs and lets me go. "It hasn't been the same since you left."

"What have I missed?"

This causes Paisley to burst out laughing. "Besides Wilder stalking her, then nothing really."

I arch an eyebrow at Joslyn, who blushes. "He just follows me to make sure I am safe."

"Liam?"

My head whips around at Paisley's voice, and I see a very tall and large man step into the bakery. I guess this is Liam. Paisley runs around the counter into his arms and wraps her legs around his waist.

He holds her tight to his body, his eyes closed tightly. "I missed you!"

My nose burns with tears and Joslyn hugs me. Joslyn is crying into my shoulder. She is a huge softy when it comes to all things love.

"How long do you have, Liam?"

"A week."

"Paisley, take the day off," I tell her and she mouths "thank you" to me and climbs down off of Liam.

"Oh, let me grab my stuff from the back." She runs out of the room, and Liam takes me in. I can tell he is younger than I am, but he has a rough-around-the-edges look and is growing his tattoos.

I step closer to him. "Don't break her heart, Liam."

He looks at the door Paisley disappeared through. "That will never fucking happen." His voice is deep. "Once I am out, I am coming for her. I will not date her over a fucking letter, she needs something more than that."

"I respect that." I step behind the counter.

Paisley emerges from the other room and waves at us, and Liam holds the door open for her. His head tilts to the side as he checks out her ass as she walks past. I grab my pen out of its holder and I throw it—I hit him on the top of his head.

He gives me a look and I arch my eyebrows. "Eyes up," I yell and he shakes his head.

Joslyn laughs and moves to the back of the bakery. I feel protective over both Paisley and Joslyn. Joslyn is literally the sweetest person I have met, and I want her to be happy.

The bell above the door rings, and some customers walk in.

"I just locked up, I will be home in a bit," I tell Butcher over the phone, and I hear Tiana laugh in the background. I can't wait to see her. I miss her like crazy. Hell, I miss them both.

I pull out of my parking lot, and Joslyn goes in the other direction toward her house. I pull into town, and I crank the radio up and roll my windows down, letting the evening air run through my hair.

Fifteen minutes later I drive by the park just outside of town. I see a Great Dane lying on the ground and a man standing beside him. The man kicks him in the stomach.

Oh my god!

I park right beside the man, who is still kicking his dog. "What the fuck are you doing?" I scream and the man glares at me.

Fuck this shit. I take my gun from my back holster, pull back the clip, and point it at him. "Get the fuck out of here before I blow your brains out."

He looks to his dog and to me, and he runs away. I open my door and bend down next to the dog, who is very skinny and looks like it's been abused for a while. My heart breaks when he looks at me with his sad eyes.

Lane has been searching for a Great Dane, and I know he will take him in. There is a vet's office right around the corner.

I open my back door and I slowly lift the dog, which takes a lot of my strength. The dog stands on shaky feet, and I lead him to the backseat. He climbs in and slumps over slightly.

I hurry to the vet's office around the corner.

I park and I see someone in a white coat locking up. Oh no. I hurry over to her. "Are you guys closing?" I ask her.

She turns around and smiles at me. If I were a lesbian, I would be pounding on her door. She is fucking gorgeous. "Yes, is everything okay?"

I explain what I came across, and she gasps and runs over to my car, opens the back door, and looks at the dog. She feels his sides and legs. "His leg is broken. I can feel that. Want to help me carry him in?"

Together we carry the dog inside, which is a huge feat in itself. We settle him down on the floor, because if we put him on an exam table, we wouldn't be able to get him back down.

"I will be right outside."

She nods and starts examining the dog.

I take my phone out and dial Lane.

"Hey, Shaylin."

"So I know you have been searching for a Great Dane, and you wanted a shelter dog."

"Yeah. You found one?"

"Sort of." I explain the situation, and he laughs when I tell him how I confronted the guy.

"Butcher is going to let you have it."

"Whatever."

He is quiet for a moment. "Tell the vet I will take care of all the bills. Give her my info?"

"I will. Thank you, Lane."

I shoot Butcher a quick text telling him I am going to be a bit late.

I walk back inside the office, and I see her giving the dog a shot. "My brother wants the dog and asked me to tell you he will cover the costs of everything."

"Don't worry about the cost, but I am glad he will have a home once he is better. He should be ready to go in a few days. He only has a broken bone in the leg, and he is way underweight, but he will fully recover." She moves over to a table and takes out a piece of paper. "Write down your brother's info, and I will give him a call once he is ready to go."

I write down Lane's name and number along with mine. I hand her the paper, and she smiles at me.

Hmm.

Lane and her?

I hide my smile. "I better go, my man is going to be pissed if he finds out I confronted the guy."

She laughs. "Don't feel bad. I saw a man throw a cat. I picked up a piece of wood and knocked him out."

She is totally perfect for Lane. I throw my head back laughing because I can just see her doing that. She is smaller than me. I am five three and she has to be like five one. She has auburn hair and large blue-green eyes.

"See you later!" I call over my shoulder and walk out the door.

I arrive home, and I am met by Butcher at the door. He is standing with his arms crossed across his chest, glaring at me.

"What is it?" I ask.

"Lane called."

It's official: I am going to kill my brother! I was going to tell Butcher, but I wanted to give him a blowjob first to soften him up. Ha! I snort at my own inside joke.

"Baby, what was I supposed to do? Let him get away with it?" I give him my most sweet and innocent look.

He rolls his eyes. "That doesn't get you out of trouble."

He steps away from the door, and I walk inside. I hear little feet running from the living room, and Tiana comes around the corner. "Mommy!" she yells and runs toward me, her arms up in the air.

I almost collapse on the ground at her saying "Mommy." Did she just say that? Did I imagine it? Her little body slams into mine, her arms going around my neck as she hugs me tightly. I look at Butcher in amazement.

"She called me 'Daddy' earlier. Adeline read her a story about parents adopting a baby, and I guess she connected the dots."

A tear slips from my eye and I close my eyes, just holding her. I hold my daughter. My hand strokes the back of her head. Is this even real? Am I dreaming this? Can life get any more perfect?

twenty-one

Shaylin

Whack! I am bent over Butcher's leg, and he is spanking me. Literally spanking me. I laugh out loud and he does it again. I laugh again while squirming, trying to get away.

"Are you going to be good?" he asks.

"No." I chuckle. "I am going to be very bad."

My comment throws him off, and I get away. I push him down onto the bed. We are both already naked.

"Fuck my face," I say.

I climb on the bed so my head is propped up on the pillows. I don't have a gag reflex, and it comes in handy in situations like this.

Butcher growls loudly and scoots so he is straddling my face. I rub his balls before taking him in my hand and stroking him from top to bottom. He hisses, closes his eyes, and throws his head back.

I love that my touch alone affects him like this. I open my mouth and place the tip inside it. I suck hard and he almost comes off the bed. I drag my nails from his thighs up to his butt, and I squeeze and pull him down, taking all of him.

"FUCK!" He grabs the headboard.

I swallow and I choke slightly. Butcher pulls out and I pull him back in. He takes my cues and starts fucking my face. I press my tongue on the underside of him, and he goes faster. I watch his face as he loses every ounce of control he has. A minute later I grab his butt again, halting his movement. I swallow over and over and over.

"Shay," he growls and he comes.

Oh yeah, I got it.

He slides out and I let him go with a pop. He grabs my feet and pulls me off the pillows. He climbs between my legs and he slams home.

"Yes!" I hiss.

He pounds into me harder and harder until the only thing I know is Butcher and the intense feeling happening between my legs. His teeth nibble at the side of my neck and I raise my legs, locking them behind his butt to push him harder into me.

"Fucking made for me," he growls and gives me a deep, wet kiss. He slows down and rises on his elbows, which are on either side of my face. "Made for me," he repeats. He slowly moves inside me and my toes curl. "I love you, my Shay."

"I love my Butcher."

He grins and presses his forehead against mine. I grip the back of his neck, holding him to me. We come together as one, staring deep into each other's eyes.

"I have nightmares that this is a dream," Butcher whispers and my heart breaks a little at his words. His dark eyes look deep into mine, his face scarred up and beautiful.

"It's real. I am real." I take his hand and press it to my heart. "This is yours."

"I don't deserve you, my Shay. But I am selfish and will take you any way I can."

I shake my head furiously and grip his face between my hands. "I am the one who doesn't deserve you, Butcher." I kiss him deeply before placing my face in the crook of his neck. I feel Butcher relax into me and I close my eyes.

Butcher is something I never thought I would have. Waiting was worth it.

A loud piercing scream has me shooting up in bed. I look around wide eyed, and I see Butcher has his boxers on and is out of bed. He leaves the room. I jump out of bed and toss on some clothes. I rush out of the room and into Tiana's. I feel panic starting to take hold.

I look around the room frantically, and I relax when I see Butcher holding Tiana. "Nightmare." I walk over to them and sink down on the floor in relief.

I take the small throw blanket and cover her up, and she raises her head and looks at me. I kiss her small cheek. "Sleep, angel. We are here." She closes her eyes and fists the blanket. Once she is asleep Butcher gently lays her back in her bed and brings her blanket up to her chest.

I stand up and Butcher follows me out of her room. I leave her door and ours open in case she gets scared again. I sink into bed and curl into Butcher.

We fall back asleep, but I have an uneasy feeling.

Another piercing scream shatters me out of my dream, and I hear feet running toward our room. Butcher jumps out of bed, and runs to the door.

Tiana is crying and Butcher picks her up. She sobs into his shoulder. Why is she having these nightmares? Butcher sits down on the edge of the bed, and I scoot over next to him. "Shh, angel, it's okay." I rub her back and she starts to settle down.

"Let her sleep with us."

Butcher lies down on his back with her on his chest, and he looks concerned. I hate that she has these dreams and they affect her this way.

An hour later she falls back asleep, and Butcher lays her on the bed between us. I bring the blanket up, covering her. She rolls over and cuddles into Butcher's side. She feels safe around him. She looks so tiny lying against his side like that.

"I will ask Myra if these dreams are normal tomorrow," I whisper and he nods. I sink down on the pillow and kiss the back of his hand, letting him know it will be okay. I can feel the worry radiating off of him.

Tiana has been through a lot, and I don't want to admit that those dreams are a part of the bad times in her life. I don't really want to think of what all she has seen. Lexi probably traumatized her, and her father is also a basket case.

I wish I could take it away from her.

I look at her tiny face, lean down, and kiss her forehead. I want to take away everything that bothers her. She was put into our lives for a reason. She is my daughter. She is mine to raise into a beautiful strong young woman who will take on the world.

I put the dishes in the dishwasher after breakfast while singing along to "Monsters" by Katie Sky. This song is perfect—it's like it was made for Butcher and me. I close the dishwasher door and

I turn around, running smack dab into Butcher's chest. He takes hold of my forearms, steadying me. His hands wrap around my back, he lifts me off the ground, and my feet rest on top of his.

"What are you doing?" I ask.

His hands slide up my back to my arms, and he lifts my hands to his shoulders. "Dancing with you."

Oh my god.

He brings his hands back down, and they rest on my ass cheeks. I roll my eyes at him. I've got to admit Butcher is super romantic when he wants to be. I rest my cheek on his shoulder, my arms wrapped around his neck, his hands on my ass. He dances us around the kitchen.

There aren't any words spoken. It is just us sharing a moment. Butcher showing another side of him—at every turn he does something that surprises me.

"Daddy!" Tiana calls. She is standing a few feet away from us, staring. She walks over to me, raising her arms. Butcher tightens his grip on me, and I pick her up and place her on my hip. Butcher smiles down at her with pure love, and that takes my breath away.

"My girls." He kisses the top of her head and then my lips. Butcher bends over, dipping us both. I laugh and she laughs along with me. Butcher dances us all over the kitchen, dipping us at different times, making Tiana squeal with laughter.

I stare at Butcher as he watches Tiana, laughing in pure amazement. How blessed am I?

twenty-two

Shaylin

One Week Later

My phone buzzes in my pocket—it's from the vet. We've been texting on and off throughout the day. We have plans next week to get lunch. She also had to keep the dog for an extra couple of days because of a cut under his leg. Lane is coming today to pick up the dog.

Amelia: Thank you
Me: Huh?
Amelia: Your brother.

I put my phone back in my pocket and laugh. Butcher will be here any minute. We are having a date night, and Adeline is babysitting.

I see him pull up outside, and I walk over to the door and turn off all the lights. Butcher opens the door and I step out and lock it.

"Ready to go?" Butcher asks and looks me up and down.

We arrive at the restaurant, which is more laid back than our first date. We are at the place where we first met. Love at first stalk! We are seated and we go ahead with giving our order. Since we have eaten here a lot, we already know what we want. I scoot in the booth, and he slides in beside me. I grin at him then snake my hand under the table and grab his dick through his jeans. He jumps and his knee hits the table.

I fall to the side, laughing my ass off.

His hand snaking inside my leggings and inside my panties halts my laughter. He did it so fast there wasn't any way to stop him. I lean forward and push my upper body against the table.

"Butcher," I hiss and try to pull his hand out.

He doesn't move, but rubs his finger against my clit.

Oh my god. I look around the room to see if anyone notices. "Someone will see, Butcher," I whisper and his face darkens.

"You think I would allow anyone to see my woman?"

I shake my head, and he snakes a finger inside me while his thumb strokes my clit furiously. I press my face into his arm and close my eyes.

The thrill of risking getting caught makes me come a lot faster. Butcher tilts in his seat and presses my face in his neck so I am hidden from everyone. I explode around his fingers, my body shuddering and shaking. He slowly takes his fingers back.

"Here is your food."

I jump in shock and sit up. The waiter stares at me with a weird expression before looking back at Butcher. "How does everything look?"

Butcher shoots me a wink and puts the finger he had inside me in his mouth. "Delicious."

No, he didn't.

I put my hands over my face. I can feel I am blushing head to toe. I hear the waiter walk away and I drop my hands, shooting Butcher a glare. He bursts out laughing, and I put a heaping scoop of mashed potatoes in his mouth. He chokes slightly, but he quits laughing for a second. He continues laughing with his mouth closed and kisses my cheek. "You look beautiful blushing, my Shay."

Me being mad is over just like that. Who can be mad at him when he is being sweet? "Yeah, yeah." I wave it off, but I can't hide my smile. "Love you to Butcher." I don't look at him but continue eating my steak.

"Love you to my Shay."

My heart still skips a beat at the sound of him calling me "my Shay." Being around Butcher gets more intense by the day. Tiana has brought us closer than I ever thought possible. That little girl has stolen my heart. She stole it the moment she looked at me with her beautiful blue eyes.

We eat in silence, but I can feel him looking at me. He does this a lot when he doesn't think I am paying attention. He just looks at me, and I do the same to him when he isn't looking. I love to just watch him, how he is a people watcher and how he sometimes smiles but ducks his head to hide it. When Tiana calls him "Daddy," his eyes light with excitement.

He is just perfect.

A lot of people just see Butcher's rough and tough exterior. He is dangerous—don't get me wrong—but there is so much more to him that that. The way he holds me at night, calls me his Shay, and watches my every move, and how he loves me and Tiana. He always wants to protect us from everything.

Once he loves, he loves with all of his heart and soul. That is Butcher.

I get back from the bathroom, after I am done eating, and I see Butcher standing by the table waiting on me. He takes my hand and tucks me close to him. I feel his body stiffen. "Butcher, what is it?"

He looks around the restaurant, checking out every person in there. He shakes his head and looks down at me. "I just got a bad feeling."

He opens the door to the restaurant, and he all but drags me to his bike. He slips on the bulletproof jacket and helmet, lifts me on the bike, and climbs on in front of me. A chill runs up my spine and I look around the parking lot, but I don't see anything unusual going on.

Butcher starts the bike and shoots out of the parking lot. He pulls into traffic, and I look back to see two SUVs start up at the same time. I just watch, and Butcher pulls to the left toward home.

twenty-three

Shaylin

The SUVs follow us.

I don't say anything, but I turn around and sit up in my seat, covering Butcher's back.

We hit the edge of town, and the two SUVs are still following. We are now surrounded by the dark. We hit a long straight stretch, and the vehicles speed up and move up on either side of us.

This is not good.

I reach behind me and take out my gun just as the man directly beside me rolls down his window. I see a gun and so does Butcher. He guns the bike and it shoots forward, leaving them all in the dust.

We turn the curve and I realize something. I want to face this head on. I am so sick and tired of this shit! "Butcher, let's just fucking get them."

"Shaylin, no. If you weren't here."

"No." I grip his vest. "I am with you. We can't allow this to come back to Tiana."

"Fuck." He slows down. He knows I am right. The SUVs come into view. Butcher speeds off into the woods, and I let out a deep breath trying to calm my nerves.

Butcher comes to a stop, pulls me off the bike, and runs with me into the middle of the field. I take my helmet off and throw it in the direction of the bike.

The two SUVs pulling into the field illuminate us in their headlights. I grab Butcher's hand. I take my gun out of the holster and grin.

Butcher reaches into his pockets and takes out two large knives. His face changes as I watch him—he turns from my Butcher into something deadly.

The doors of the SUV open, and I pull back the clip on my gun. I turn my head, grinning at them.

The first person out of the SUV is Mary. That right there shocks the hell out of me. She is followed by five men.

"Well, if it isn't Shaylin!" Mary calls and lets out a cackle which irks my nerves right off the bat. What has Mary gotten herself into? "Who adopted my niece, Tiana?"

Butcher and I step forward at the same time when she says Tiana's name. My eyes narrow, ready to beat some ass.

Mary tilts her head and gives me a sly look. "Let me tell you a story, shall we?" She rubs her hands together. "Lexi, my dear cousin, went and got knocked up by Levi, and she didn't tell anyone. She got the little shit taken from her, and she got her life on track. Lexi didn't know I was fucking Levi. I was the fucking queen, and I was using you to spy for him. To watch the fucking MC. So you guys wouldn't fuck with his drug empire."

She sits down on the hood of the SUV. "Levi and I came up with a plan. Trafficking is some good money and I need a new car. Lexi was worthless and never took care of the kid. She was a burden and was always so needy, wanting food. Why don't we sell her? Get rid of her?"

She bangs her hand on the hood, glaring at me. "Until Lexi found out I was going to sell Tiana. She grabbed her two meth-head friends and ran, but she ran to you. She overdosed on some drugs I gave her. Then you adopted her daughter.

"Levi said he would get her back, right? The deal was still in action. Levi sent some guys. You fucking killed them, and this fucker killed Levi. These men here are hired by me to kill you guys, and I am taking Tiana. I have one day to finalize the deal, or I am dead. But guess what, Shaylin, I played you for years! I was just your friend for information! Once we got the deal for Tiana, I left your ass behind." She laughs again like a maniac.

Rage isn't the word for what I am feeling right now—it doesn't even touch the surface. I've gotten a glimpse of what Tiana had to deal with. Nobody here can fucking leave. They all must die. Butcher is so mad he is shaking. A calm comes over me and I smile at Mary, and her eyes narrow at the sight.

"You're dead." I raise my gun in a split second and pull the trigger. It seems to happen in slow motion. The bullet hits her in the center of her forehead. Her body jerks from the impact before she falls forward and hits the ground.

The five men jump into action, charging for us. Butcher pushes me back and transforms into Butcher.

He spins, bringing the knives around, and slices the first guy in the throat. He growls loudly and brings the knife up, stabbing him under the chin. He spins his torso and hits another right in the forehead. He pulls both knives from the man's head, and another man comes up behind him. Butcher spins around and brings both knives to his throat. He makes an X, slicing him from ear to ear. The last man looks at Butcher in shock and turns around to run off. Butcher throws a knife and hits him on the back of the head.

Then silence.

Butcher's back is to mine, and I am breathing heavily after everything that just happened. I can't believe Mary was going to fucking sell Tiana. The sweetest baby in the whole world. I couldn't allow her to leave. Tiana would still be in danger.

"Butcher!" I call.

He whips around, drops the knives, and runs over to me. He picks me up off the ground, and I sigh with relief when I am in his arms.

"Fucking sell my baby girl," he chokes and I nod.

I cannot even fathom what would have happened to her. I just can't.

"Let me call the guys, they will clean up. I want to go home to Tiana," I tell him.

He is on the phone for ten minutes, and I walk over to his bike. He follows me and I sink to the ground next to it.

"My poor baby." I cry.

Butcher sits down on the ground next to me, holding me tightly to him. "Mary said she was always asking for food, Butcher! They were horrible to her. My baby. My sweet angel. She was going to sell her, Butcher, she would have had god knows what done to her. Who could do that? Who is Mary?" I cry and he rocks me in his arms as he tries to soothe me.

"Butcher, they came to her, to sell her." I sob again in pure fear. "Butcher, I never thought about what she went through. They didn't care for her, she suffered her whole little life and then they were..." I can't say the words and I stuff my face into his neck, crying again. "It hurts so much. My heart." I grip his shirt and he kisses my temple. It hurts so bad, the pain I feel for her. The thought of something happening and her being neglected hurts me so much.

I love that little girl so much.

"She is with us for this reason, Shay. We were meant to protect her," Butcher tells me and I nod. We are here to take care of Tiana, to protect her and give her the best life we can.

tuenty-five

Butcher

The guys arrive once Shaylin has calmed down. I've have never felt someone's pain like I did with her. It tore me to fucking pieces seeing her like that, and I never want to see that again. Shaylin, I love her so fucking much that it hurts to breathe sometimes because the love I have is so fucking overwhelming.

I carried her into the house, once we got back, and settled her into bed. She is emotionally spent. Adeline handed me Tiana. I set her on the bed, and she curled up beside Shaylin. I see Shaylin's tears before she can hide them.

Adeline was filled in and Smiley just left with her. I crawl into bed with Tiana between me and Shaylin. I see Shaylin's shoulder shake, and I can tell many things are bothering her. Her friend Mary betraying her in such a way and, most of all, Tiana.

Tiana smiles at me and plays with Shaylin's hair. "Mommy sleep?"

Shaylin lifts her head and smiles at Tiana. She is so fucking beautiful it hurts. Tiana bends her head closer. "Cwyin?" Tiana bends her head and kisses Shaylin. "It's kay."

Shaylin pulls Tiana against her, hugging her. One hand is wrapped around her back, and the other is on the back of her head.

"This is the first moment of our forever, Butcher."

I place my hand on her cheek, catching her last tear. "My life didn't start until I met you, and my forever started the moment our baby looked me in the eye. This is the beginning of our happily ever after."

Shaylin gives me that heart-shattering smile. "To crazy, unconventional love."

I laugh and kiss her.

The END

epilogue

Four Months Later

I'm pregnant.

I put the pregnancy test down on the counter and continue to stare at it. Holy shit. I place my palm on the center of my stomach.

"Shay, want me to pick up a..." Butcher sticks his head in the door and looks from the pregnancy test to the palm that is resting on my stomach. "What is this?" he asks and steps into the room.

I hand him the digital pregnancy test, letting him see for himself. Butcher stares down at the test, completely devoid of emotion.

I let out a deep breath as I wait for what he is going to say. "My Shay is carrying *my* baby?" He finally lifts his head and looks at me.

"We've got to go to the doctor for a one hundred percent, but I skipped my period last month and also this month."

He grins at me, and a loud burst of laughter comes out of him. He splits the distance between us, and I laugh at his reaction. He pesters my face with kisses, gets down on his knees, and kisses me right below my stomach. "It's a boy."

"We don't know that for sure, Butcher." I laugh and rub the top of his head. He looks up at me, his eyes lit up with happiness.

"I know it's a boy. I feel it. We've got to have someone who can help watch over Tiana. We are going to fucking need all the help we can get."

Tiana is going to be a badass—she won't need help from any man or need protecting. Once she is old enough, she is going into karate and everything else she possibly can to protect herself. There are too many fucking people that are crazy in this world, and anyone can betray you—my thoughts drift back to Mary.

"I am so fucking happy, my Shay," he whispers.

"Me too."

Life just gets better and better. Butcher gets more amazing by the day, and Tiana is growing every day, getting sassier every second. She has Butcher wrapped around her little finger and is a total daddy's girl through and through.

Delivery Day

"Push!" a male nurse yells, and I push with all of my might, screaming. Zach has a huge head or something. I was told he was a big baby, and I fucking believe it.

"Harder!" he screams again, getting on my last nerve. I open my eyes and glare at him.

Butcher steps toward him. "If you don't shut the fuck up, I am going to knock you the fuck out."

My dad, who is on the other side of me, laughs.

Another contraction hits and I grip the blanket. Butcher growls loudly and paces the side of my bed. Butcher has been in a fit ever since I had the first contraction. I don't think he realized that it would hurt or something. He has been ready to murder someone.

I push again, and Dad and Butcher hold my legs back. I know it's not normal having your dad in the delivery room with you, but he has been my mom and dad.

I let out a deep breath and collapse on the bed. "We are never having another kid, Shaylin. I can't stand that you are in fucking pain." He punches the wall.

"I think I need to call security," a nurse whispers, and Butcher's head whips around like the girl in *The Exorcist*. "I dare you to make me leave. Dare you!"

Dad and I both laugh at that. I love that man.

A contraction hits again, and I push with all of my might. "I see the head! One more push!" I grab the rails of the bed and scream as I give one final push.

They place the baby on my stomach, and I burst out crying at the sight of my baby boy. Butcher bends down next to me to look at him. He is perfect. He has a large amount of black hair, just like Butcher.

"Zack," Butcher whispers and his eyes are full of tears.

"It was more than worth it." I touch Zack's little hand and then they take him away.

"It was, but we aren't having another one. You are not going through that again." He steps away from the bed and follows the nurses who have Zack.

"So proud of you, baby girl." Dad kisses the top of my head and I close my eyes.

"Love you, Dad."

I wake up a few hours later and see Butcher fast asleep with Zack resting on his chest. The door opens and a nurse pops in. She looks at me and Butcher.

"We can take him to the nursery so you guys can get some rest?" She holds out her arms to take Zack.

"We are fine. He doesn't leave us."

Butcher is ever the protective father, and I am the same. We don't trust anyone outside of our circle. We keep people who aren't in the MC at arm's length until we know them.

"Okay, I understand." She smiles at both of us and checks the monitors. Zack starts crying, and Butcher lays him gently on my chest. I pull down my gown so he can breastfeed. Butcher gently sets the boppy pillow under Zack to help me hold him. I am weak.

"I wonder what Zack is going to be when he grows up?" I stare down at him, and I can't believe I carried him for nine months. Butcher and I made him, and he is so precious. I cannot wait for Tiana to see him.

Tiana is three years old now. She is getting big so fast. She says full sentences now and is so smart. She doesn't like dolls or princesses now. No, she likes tearing things apart and putting them back together.

"Tiana will be a mechanic, and Zack can be whatever the hell he wants to be."

"No sex for six weeks."

He drops his head to the bed. "Don't remind me."

I laugh and take his hand, which is resting on my leg. I bring it up and kiss the back of it.

"Love you, Butcher."

He raises his head and gives me a lazy smile. "Love you too, Momma."

Tiana Starts Kindergarten

"Butcher, she is fine," I whisper to him for the tenth time. He is looking through the door window. We just dropped Tiana off for her first day of school.

"That little boy beside her is offering her a pencil. She is too young, we know little boys don't give a pencil for no reason."

Oh my god. He is crazy! I burst out laughing, and Zack laughs along with me. He walks over to Butcher and raises his arms for Butcher to pick him up. Butcher picks him up and goes back to staring through the window. "What if she gets hungry, Shay?"

"Butcher, we have packed her a lunch," I inform him.

"Maybe we can homeschool her?"

I roll my eyes and physically drag him from the door. "Butcher, she is fine. I promise. All of the other MC kids go here also."

He nods and takes one long look before he walks away. He stops a few times before continuing. It's taking everything in him not to turn around. Butcher is a very protective dad—it messes with him when they are out of his sight. It fucks with him, the thought of something going wrong and not being there.

He is better with it when family babysits, but he just left her with a strange teacher and aide. We know this school. It's out of town, very small and out of the way. All of the MC go here. We have hired full-time security with the school's permission.

"I know, Shay. I love that little shit in there."

I laugh and hug his side. "She loves you too, Butcher, and she will be waiting for us to pick her up later."

"Let's stay around town today."

Zachary, Fifteen Years Old

"Mom, Zach is on the roof shooting leaves off of trees again," Tiana informs me and I spin around.

I am still taken aback by her beauty. When I say puberty hit her, I mean it hit her so fucking hard. She is drop-dead gorgeous, which Butcher cannot stand. Boys knock on our gate asking her out daily. Tiana has a voice-automated thing set up telling them no and wishing them luck with someone else.

Tiana isn't interested in boys. She is interested in cars and being a mechanic. She is damn good at it too—she can fix anything.

"This kid lives to give me a heart attack. I swear." I throw the dishtowel down and stomp outside to the porch. I crane my head back and look to the roof.

"Zack, if you don't get your butt down, you're never leaving your room again besides school. That means no outdoor activities, no nothing."

He pops his head over the side of the roof. "You mean I can't even get married?"

"Yes. Down!" I point to the ground.

He climbs down and lands beside me. "Mom, I want to get married someday!" he jokes with a little smirk.

"You're my baby boy—you are never getting married." I grab his hand and pull him to me. I pester his face with kisses and he laughs.

"There is this boy in my class who will make anyone think of getting married. His name is Xavier."

I freeze. Did he say "boy"? I pull back and look him dead in the eye. "Boy?"

He shrugs. "Yeah, Mom, I like boys." His eyes widen nervously, and I pull him into a hug. "Well, at least we ain't going to have to worry about teenage pregnancy."

He laughs and I let him go. I don't care if my kid likes boys or girls. It's his life, love is love, and he can love whoever he wants.

"I am going to tell Dad tonight."

Butcher

"Dad, can I talk to you?" My son could pass for my twin at that age. He has his mother's heart-stopping smile, but the rest is me.

"Yeah." I nod at the seat beside me, and I can see he is fidgeting. My eyes narrow as I look him over, wondering what is wrong.

He sits down and lets out a deep breath. "So I have something to tell you, I told Mom earlier."

I sit forward and it's fucking getting to me seeing him nervous.

"I'm gay."

Fuck me. Is that it? I look at him, confused. "Is that it?"

Zach's mouth pops open. "Yeah, that's it."

"Okay, who cares if you like dick?"

He drops his head, his face red with embarrassment. "Dad." He laughs.

"About time you told them!" Tiana comes into the room. "I figured it out a long time ago." She walks to a closet door and peers inside. "I was like, every day, you coming out? No? Okay. Took long enough, bro." She smiles and walks over to him, bends down, and hugs him. "Love you."

I did a good fucking job raising these kids. I feel someone beside me, and I look over to see Shaylin staring at them both with tears in her eyes.

"We did good."

"We did, My Shay." I kiss her on the lips.

This may be the end of our story, but it isn't for our kids.

They will find their own crazy.

acknowledgements

Lydia my wonderful Publicist and PA, where do I start with you? You have been my life line through this whole entire book and without you I would have went crazy a long time ago. Thank you for everything you do!

My readers, thank you so much! You guys are the best. <3

My Review Team: You guys are my biggest support system and push me to be better with every book. You also never hesitate to give me words of encouragements.

about the author

LeAnn Asher's is a blogger turned author who released her debut novel early 2016 and can't wait to see where this new adventure takes her. LeAnn writes about strong-minded females and strong protective males who love their women unconditionally.

Website: https://authorleannashers.com
Facebook: https://www.facebook.com/LeAnnashers
Instagram: https://www.instagram.com/leann_ashers/
Twitter: https://twitter.com/LeannAshers
Goodreads:
https://www.goodreads.com/author/show/14733196.LeAnn_A
shers
Amazon: https://www.amazon.com/LeAnn-
Ashers/e/B01AVUCOLG

More from LeAnn Ashers

Forever Series

Protecting His Forever
Loving His Forever

Devil Souls MC Series

Torch
Techy
Butcher
Liam

Grim Sinners MC Series

Lane
Wilder

Made in the USA
Coppell, TX
23 February 2020

16109151R00115